Skin Deep Motives

Blinking at an opaque mist that was creeping into my peripheral vision, I peered around the main lobby, then stumbled against the arboretum, pressing my palms against the glass for balance. As I scanned the lobby slowly in search of a sign indicating the restrooms, a gang of tattooed Goths floated past me like apparitions, ignoring my pleas for help.

I gaped as the ink burst out of their skins in blots and swirls. U of O's green and yellow Fighting Duck on a dude's massive biceps heckled me with quacks. Chinese throwing stars popped from a bed of lotus blossoms decorating another guy's sleeve to twirl at my head. I raised my arms to block, bent my knees to dodge. Cruel laughter flooded my ears, drawing me down a discombobulating whirlpool. A fairy pinup sporting a flailing dragon's tail on a girl's lower back winked, then toasted me with a sip from a martini in its taloned hand. The liquid spewed back out in a singeing flame.

Pepper's face appeared in my hallucinogenic haze, her expression terrified. "What the hell's wrong with you?"

"Drugged, poisoned," I rasped. "Need to get—emergency room . . ."

SKIN DEEP MOTIVES

AARON HILTON

PORTLAND, OREGON

A BACKWATER CRIME BOOK

Second paperback edition: May 2013

Copyright © 2012 by Aaron Hilton

Edited by Marg Fleming Gilks
Cover art by Carl Graves
Backwater Crime logo and illustration by Daniel Cooney
Author photograph by Angelique Herrington
Featuring Melissa Kate as The Muse

ISBN 978-0-9853941-2-7

For Earl Shea
February 16, 1942-October 31, 2010
Encouragement bestowed.

Skin Deep Motives

Prologue

Matt Grudge

I REGAINED consciousness to a burning throb in my biceps and shoulders. My lungs pressed against battered ribs, shooting sharp bursts of pain through my chest with every breath I drew. I tasted copper inside a mouth lacerated raw, much like the wrists that chafed within handcuffs.

The bright light from a fluorescent beam struck me in the face and lingered, pulling me out of my fog. I took stock of my condition. Working my jaw sent a warm mouthful of blood and saliva dribbling down my chin. I opened my left eye slowly, painfully, my right too swollen to operate.

Dark shadows materialized in the light. The drug I'd been slipped still had such a distorting effect on my sight that my abductors morphed from one person to sometimes three. The knockout drug also screwed with my hearing, making it difficult to comprehend what they were saying.

Until my attention fixed on another threat.

" . . . that Pocahontas bitch you run with can't save you, or herself, now. We know she's close to mounting a rescue. An assassin on our payroll will shred her to pieces."

I tried to stall them. I moaned the opening chords of "Come As You Are," the last thing I remembered hearing before I couldn't defend myself in the ambush.

"This cat thinks he's got lives left," one of my attackers noted, laughing.

"You dumb son of a bitch," an accomplice said. "I told you not to give him too strong a dose."

"Would you both shut your mouths and relax," a feminine, whiskey-soaked voice with a Dutch accent said. "He's just pretending to be a vegetable to bide time. Zap him."

My head snapped back and I screamed into wooden rafters as a charge of electricity coursed from my navel out through my muscles and nerve endings. The jolt stopped, leaving my naked body swinging back and forth like a metronome. The vibrations of my torment spooked a horse nearby, and it kicked anxiously at its stall a few times.

"Good," the throaty-sounding dominatrix drawled in approval. "Next time he doesn't answer correctly, hit him for a full minute. Matthew, can you hear me?"

I lifted my head long enough to nod, then grinned, more a snarl. "I've had tattoos hurt worse than anything you can do to me," I said, spitting blood.

"Charming. Apart from Leslie, who else knows about my operation?"

"Operation?" I gurgled, a stream of snot oozing from my nostril. I mulled over my response for a minute. How the hell did a covered-up murder turn into an *operation*? I might

4

survive long enough to find out, if I played it stubborn and pretended to know more than I actually did.

"Well? I'm waiting, Matthew."

"You threatened a friend of mine," I said. "An artist I've sworn to protect. Suck. My. Tattooed. Dick."

I screamed some more as the electrodes were held against my genitals this time, for a full minute. My sweaty body sizzled like bacon frying. One of the fillings in my mouth snapped off and I swallowed it. I gagged and lost my bladder control.

"Ah, shit!" one lackey complained. "He pissed on my suit. May I be excused so I can clean up?"

"Yes, but come right back."

I heard the flick of a lighter, then smelled the rich tobacco scent of a cigarette that couldn't be domestic.

"There are infinite ways I can make you suffer," the bitch said. "I can cut you a thousand times, but the last thing I want is to mutilate the artwork on your body. Maybe I'll rip the piercings out of your face and nipples. You have until I finish this smoke to furnish the names, then I'm going to plug the juice in until your eyeballs *pop*."

Shutting my left eye tight, I tried to block out the pain and the sound of the horse's increasingly agitated neighs.

One

Matt Grudge

ALMOST THIRTY-TWO hours earlier, the police scanner mounted on the bookshelf behind my desk next to my camera gear and a dog-eared copy of *In Cold Blood* crackled. The dispatcher broadcasted a robbery homicide. Springing forward in the chair too fast, I scalded my hand with coffee.

"Ouch, shit."

I swung my feet off my desk with more care and tossed the report I'd been proofreading on the ring-stained oak surface. Setting the mug down (carefully this time), I dashed into the outer office.

Leslie had already pulled on her coat. She flung my worn-out jacket at my head. "Move it, Matt."

She was halfway to the elevator when I paused to dead-bolt the frosted glass door emblazoned with *Alternative Investigations —Matt Grudge & Leslie Crow.*

"What's your damn hurry?" I said, tightening my seatbelt as Leslie raced her midnight blue Saturn over the Morrison Bridge crossing the murky Willamette River. "The crime scene isn't going anywhere."

"Quit griping," she told me. "You want firsthand information, or do you want to read about it? Hold on."

Leslie threaded her way through traffic as if she were navigating a raceway. Horns blared and tooted. "What the hell are you doing?" I shouted over the motorists' horns as she reached inside her jacket pocket, pulled out her cell phone, and balanced the handset at twelve o'clock on the steering wheel. "You're gonna get us pulled over—or killed," I complained, but her thumbs kept tapping out a text message.

The horn blaring behind us didn't stop. Leslie's eyes darted to the rearview mirror. She'd swerved into the right lane too quickly and hadn't spotted the Thunderbird LX speeding up. Spinning the wheel, she floored the gas to pass a tow truck, then cut in front of it to let the T-bird shoot past.

"You crazy bitch," the truck driver yelled out as the truck's brakes squealed like pigs being butchered.

The light at Grand clicked to yellow. Leslie blasted through the intersection and a huge puddle of water from an overflowed drain. A guy outside the Dutch Brothers coffee stand got drenched.

"Assholes!"

The time on the stereo read twenty minutes past six as Daria O' Neill's sexy purr on the Buzz issued an evening news update. *"Commuters in Southeast will want to avoid Morrison Street between Grand and Sixth Avenue,"* the radio entertainer advised. *"PPD has barricaded that area and detoured nighttime rush hour over to Stark."*

Leslie hung a left on Belmont into the Bank of America parking lot behind the Weatherly Building, a hop and a skip away from the crime scene.

"Any clues as to what's happened?" Daria's co-star, Mitch, asked in his deep, resonant voice.

She exuded Lauren Bacall over the airwaves. *"I've made a few subtle inquiries. Apparently, several uniformed officers and plain clothes detectives have been sighted entering and exiting the Femme Ink Piercing and Tattoo Parlor at 611 Southeast Morrison."*

Their producer, Ted, commented that calls pouring into the studio had just become a flood. Listeners were offering or requesting more information about what'd happened.

"Thank you for your concern, folks. But even if we were privy to more details," Mitch said, *"we definitely wouldn't release any without permission. It would sensationalize the crime and that's the last thing we'd ever want—"*

I switched the stereo off before Leslie pulled into a space and cranked the ignition off.

"Something's going on," she said, her half-blooded Lakota Sioux features brooding. "Dee answers my texts faster than this." Pocketing her phone, she pulled her long, jet-black hair up underneath a Winterhawks baseball cap. The drizzling rain had turned into a downpour.

We climbed out of the Saturn. Slamming her door shut, Leslie activated the car alarm, then rushed off. I dashed after her, grabbed her shoulder, and turned her around.

"Take it easy. I'm sure nothing's wrong," I said in an undertone. "Dee-Dee's probably just got her hands full, giving the cops a statement."

Leslie's lips curled in disdain. "Maybe I should punch you in the gut to show you how I'm feeling?"

The twelve-storey Weatherly Building loomed behind us, a symbol of the business world that would never assimilate two private detectives who did most of their investigating wearing piercings, tattoos, and vintage clothing from clearance racks. We always seemed like round pegs trying to fit into square holes. A frequent joke whispered behind our backs was that we were a pair of low-rent losers too lazy to reinvent our image beyond the nineties. Which always seemed funny to me, living in Portland, a town chock full of throwback fashions, including the nineties, eighties, seventies, and sixties. I mean, why pick on the nineties?

Point is, I knew exactly how she felt. Like shit. Underrated, unappreciated, disillusioned shit.

"Next time we're at the gym, you're on," I said. "With pads or without?"

Leslie slugged me on the shoulder. "Keep up, wise-ass."

At the intersection, a drenched, uniformed policewoman stood between a pair of sawhorses with twirling lights, redirecting traffic with her waving nightstick and harsh toots on her whistle. Passing behind the barricade, we stepped up onto the sidewalk in front of the Sixth Avenue Grocery and Deli's barred windows.

Out of earshot from the horde of journalists and photographers huddled around Femme Ink, I voiced a fond memory to cheer up Leslie. "This is the joint where you dragged me to get my first tat."

"Yeah," she said, releasing a chuckle. "The only other time I heard you swear so much was the first time you got shot—"

"Hey!" a geeky voice shrilled. "It's the Grunge Operatives. Have you been called in to consult on the investigation?"

It was Derek Sharp, a paparazzi infamous for scavenging on suspects and victims like a vulture. He maintained a monetized (porn site-financed) true-crime blog that fed a frenzied media scraps of false information. Sharp was clever, though, so a lawsuit for libel hadn't shut him down.

"What aspects of this case has Chief Burden shared that require the attention of your specialized trade?" Sharp asked in a nasal voice caused by the nose splint he frequently wore. He thrust an MP3 recorder at our faces. "Comment," the prick said. "People have a right to know."

I shoved his fleshy shoulder lightly aside so we could squeeze around him. "Truth is, Sharp, Leslie and I are just hanging out to observe the activities of a certain blogger."

"Yeah," Leslie said, picking up on my comment as if via ESP. "We want to see whether his nose gets broken again for sniffing around where it doesn't belong, or if we can gather proof to bust his ass for extortion and fraud."

Ignoring the disparaging comment, Sharp tagged behind us like a leech. "I can see the post heading now: Grunge Ops Seek

Femme Ink Killer," he said, holding the MP3 recorder between my right shoulder and Leslie's poker face.

I almost warned the prick that if I heard him say that nickname again, I'd put him through one of the nearby windows, but I didn't need to; rage was building inside Leslie. Her breasts weren't rising and falling with even breathing.

As Sharp fired off more questions with the staccato rhythm of a machine gun, Leslie's shoulders flinched. She was about to launch a fist, or an elbow, at Sharp's mouth. I peered down at her hands. Leslie stuffed them into her skin-tight jean pockets and met my sideways glance with a yearning that said, *I so much want to deck this asshole.*

We reached the rearmost reporters in the gang that bordered the entrance to Femme Ink.

"Hey, Leslie," Sharp said, "if I can't gather enough details for a post about what's gone down in this dump, maybe the picture I just took of your fine ass can *splash* a column about local female celebrities who could make a living as strippers. What would your stage name be?"

When Sharp thrust his MP3 out, I put a Greco-Roman wrestling hold on his wrist. He winced in pain. His fingers uncurled. The MP3 recorder fell to the asphalt. "Enough, jackass," I said, letting him go. "Respect my partner's space."

"My bad," he said with mock sincerity.

Massaging his aching wrist, Sharp bent over to retrieve his recorder, but Leslie's riding boot kicked it under the trampling feet of the mob. "Oops," she said, a wide grin parting her lips. The silver hoop in her upper lip glimmered above whitened teeth.

"You cunt," Sharp hissed.

Leslie drove every muscular pound built by her free-weight training into an uppercut. Sharp's jaw slammed his bottom lip into his teeth, and a trail of bloody spittle spewed across the parlor window, marring the display of poster boards showing flash—standard designs the artists in Femme Ink tattooed frequently. I watched Sharp's blood run down the image of a Celtic cross tombstone on which a crow perched, wings spread, beak open.

Then I caught the unconscious paparazzi under his arms and lowered him to slump beneath the window. "Niiice shot. I think you were holding back, though. Go ahead, hit him again."

"Shut up," Leslie said, shaking her scuffed knuckles.

For some comic relief, I grabbed a discarded plastic cup and wrapped the news panhandler's fingers around it. I even snatched a handful of change from my pocket and dumped it into the cup to get him started.

We rejoined the cluster of reporters and found a vantage point everyone else was avoiding, a space by a garbage can and a recycling bin that stank of rotting produce. I scanned the crowd, which was busy questioning patrol officers and detectives entering, exiting, or milling about. Hearing rummaging behind me, I turned as Leslie kicked a sturdy apple crate over and stepped up onto it so she could stand shoulder-to-shoulder with me to study the crowd.

Besides newshounds nosing for a scoop, the crime scene had attracted cosmopolitan groups of people. My eyes drifted over the skirted business suits on a pair of bank tellers who'd forgotten to take off their name tags. Leslie cleared her throat and elbowed me to make sure I didn't stare at their firm, nylon-clad legs too long.

I spotted a stout Hindustani man sporting an immaculate haircut underneath a blue and white beach umbrella he shared with a journalist scribbling notes. The Indian gentleman—Bob—released one hand from the umbrella he was clutching against the wind whirling around the Weatherly Building to wave politely. I nodded back, suppressing a grimace. Bob the barber had been cutting my hair since I was in junior high. His shop sat next door to the B of A. A gust of wind almost yanked the umbrella out of his grip. Rainwater spilled over the edge of the umbrella to douse the newspaperman's notes.

Skaters in baggy, shredded jeans hung out next to him, their sleeveless denim jackets showing off their tats, their pierced baby faces solemn. A cameraman hefted a video camera on his shoulder and a reporter on Bob's right was muttering into a mini-cassette recorder.

Three men in suits huddled between them, making me think of pallbearers for a funeral. Their features were eastern European, as were the expensive cuts and threads of their clothes. A bald-headed one mouthed words into a Bluetooth he could've purchased at Tiffany's—the accessory was studded with diamonds. The words I watched him mumble needed subtitles.

Bumps underneath their clothes revealed that they hadn't provided their tailor with explicit firearm measurements.

Two patrolmen joined the two officers that'd been guarding the corridor of yellow and black *Crime Scene—Do Not Cross* tape leading up to the entrance of Femme Ink. The four enforcers walked both sides of the crowd back, firmly commanding, "Step back please, folks. Step back, or you'll be ordered to disperse."

I craned my head and shoulders around, careful not to knock Leslie from her perch, and sighted a '57 Chevy pickup with peeling white paint driving through the maze of unmarked cars and cruisers. The back of the rig wreaked of fish. A rack mounted in the cab's rear window was stocked with fishing poles.

The relic lurched to a hard stop. Martin Goldman hopped from the cab, dressed in faded black jeans and a plaid flannel shirt, his greasy salt-and-pepper hair under a blue baseball cap adorned with flies and lures and embroidered silver letters that read ME. His trademark ponytail dangling through the back of the cap flopped around like a horse's tail.

He stopped near the entrance to sign a log one of the patrolmen held steady, then snapped on a pair of latex gloves over his filthy hands, and hunkered down to pull a pair of booties over his boots. When Goldman straightened to his full height to enter the parlor a couple of head lengths away, I didn't need to shout.

"Interrupt your fishing trip, Marty?" I asked.

His head spun around, pointing a red, unshaven face and bulldog nose my way. "Don't call me that," he snapped automatically. "Who—oh, it's you, Grudge. I almost didn't see you. You blend in like a permanent fixture next to that trashcan. Perfect."

I gave the ME a dumb smirk as he entered the crime scene. A wide stream of brown water and soggy leaves from a clogged gutter splashed my shoulder.

Leslie sniffled and wiped her runny nose with the back of her hand.

Going on two hours and about an inch of rainfall later, EMTs wheeled a gurney into Femme Ink. About thirty minutes after that, they wheeled the body out. The department's supply of body bags must have been depleted; the victim was covered with a sheet.

How could transporting the body get any worse? None of the unmarked cars or cruisers were moved for the ambulance to park in closer.

The gurney wheels hit the street at an awkward angle. The sheet came untucked. One of the medics leapt to grab a corner of the cotton shroud and hold it in place, but wind from the gorge whipped it free, and the body jostled under his weight, allowing the victim's hand to fall out into view.

Leslie squinted almond-shaped eyes, then jumped down off the apple box and trotted around the mob of news jackals the uniformed officers held back from the gurney. I followed closely, making sure no one knocked her down to get trampled as people thronged to envelop us.

A crowd this size was a cakewalk compared to the mosh pits in the clubs we frequented. When some guy tried to nudge her off her path, I grappled his arm, locked his elbow, then shoved him aside. Leslie ducked a microphone some female newscaster almost brained her with while launching questions.

Leslie reached the victim, pulled a latex glove out of her coat pocket, and gently touched the pale female hand, then curled the fingers inward. The long, square fingernails painted a stark red were pale in comparison to the oxidized, dark brown blood staining the sheet covering the head. "No, please God," Leslie said, her breath gusting from her mouth to fog in the cool air.

Strobe lights flashed, highlighting flaming Olde English letters tattooed on the knuckles.

F-I-R-E

Leslie shut her eyes tight for a moment and bowed her head.

The woman's right hand belonged to Dee-Dee Magnolia, a local celebrity tattoo artist. The bottled-blonde had taken third place at Bathing Beauties In Ink, a regional beauty contest for tattoo aficionados, last spring. The winner had to display the greatest number of tattoos visible in the skimpiest bikini or thong imaginable. Second went to the Suicide Girls, first to Kat Von D.

"Oh shit," I said, remembering she was also the proprietress of Femme Ink, and Leslie's friend.

One of the paramedics slapped Leslie's hand away. "Let her go," he said, pulling the victim's hand back to tuck it into the soaked sheet. The full-color tattoos on Dee-Dee's arm showed through the sticky dampness.

Mouth sagging open, Leslie stuffed her hands into her jean pockets and stomped off through the sheets of rain. I followed after her.

The drain at the corner of the B of A was flooded. I leapt ungracefully over the swirling mess; she slogged right through up to her ankles. She increased her pace and stomped through another deep puddle in the parking lot to reach the Saturn. I jogged around to the passenger side. Wiping drops of water out of my eyes, I watched Leslie jerk at the car door handle, enraged.

"Fuck," she yelled, releasing the handle, then turning her back to lean against the door, staring back the way we'd come.

Walking around to Leslie, I stood toe to toe with her, then pulled insistently on her shoulder to bring her slowly toward me. Her body trembled with shivers that didn't come from the rain, and her eyes were hard, determined—the look I saw when she emptied her Glock on the pistol range.

"Leslie. What the hell's going on? You know something about Dee-Dee's death?"

"I'm fine," she wheezed, holding her breath.

"Give me the keys. I'm driving us home." As I reached for her jacket pocket, I saw her right shoulder pull back to throw the punch. I stepped quickly back and she only clipped my chin, then I lunged forward to wrap both arms around her.

Leslie bucked and thrashed. "Goddammit," she shouted, the rain needling the asphalt drowning out the grief in her voice, but not the erratic beat of her heart. "Let me go."

She yelled a little longer, smashing her fists against my back. The blows made me wince. I grasped the back of her neck in the bear hug and felt how frigid she was from going into shock. After about five minutes, she went limp and snuggled her face against my chest to let out a muffled wail.

"It's going to be okay," I said. "You'll be my client for this case."

•

WIPING THE sleep out of my eyes, I squinted at the time on my HP laptop. The faded display in the corner of the scraped fifteen-inch screen read half past eleven. The refurbished hand-me-down was burning through its third backlight in five years and giving me eye strain. A new computer would be nice, but the recession placed that way down the line.

I got up from the desk in my part of our spartan offices to stretch and get a coffee refill, doctoring the java with three heaping tablespoons of sugar and plenty of cream. I took a long pull, then eased down in one of the two plush, armless chairs that faced Leslie's desk. I cradled the large mug in both hands. The warmth relaxed the tension in my fingers.

I'd spent the last three hours working the phone and the Internet, searching local newsgroups and contacting discreet sources inside the Portland Police Bureau for any details about Dee-Dee's murder, but a total information blackout had been put into effect. Not even the local news at ten or eleven had reported the crime. What factors would convince the media to go to sleep on murder?

I took another sip of coffee to counteract a chill that penetrated my bones to travel along my spine, staring at the vacant chair where my partner should've been. I hoped Leslie was going to be alright. The brief discussion we had in her loft after I'd dropped her off had knocked my confidence down a couple of notches.

"Maybe you wouldn't mind spending the night at the office. I need a little space," she'd told me as she filled a kettle with water, then walked around me to get into the cupboard. She snatched a box of green tea and slammed the cherrywood door shut.

"Okay, sure," I'd said. "I'll call you tomorrow night."

"Make it Sunday morning," she'd mumbled while ripping a tea bag packet open with her teeth. "I don't know what kind of mood I'll be in if I'm unable to get ahold of Dee's family."

I wouldn't go that long without reporting to a client. She knew our profession better than that. "Leslie, you're my partner and my friend, so I'm prepared to give you as much time as you need to heal. But you're also my client now, which means I will update you nightly. That means speaking to you. I won't leave messages or send texts. And looking for you might keep the case from going forward."

"Fine. Leave me the hell alone, Matt."

Swinging my coat and rucksack full of extra clothes over my shoulder, I'd headed for the door, then turned slightly to give Leslie one last gaze of remorse.

"What? Get the fuck out of here," she said before I'd left.

Two

Leslie Crow

AFTER MATT finally stopped hovering and took a hike, I mounted a stool at the bar in the kitchen, leaned on my elbows, rubbed my temples, and breathed, so deeply that it sounded like the beat of ocean surf.

Last weekend I'd made a getaway to Newport, and Dee-Dee had accompanied me.

Grief drove blows into my stomach. I shut my eyes tight to block the pain. Tension coursed, burning through my veins and over my skin like a niacin rash. I felt my entire back itch and resisted the urge to scratch it.

Born on an Indian reservation, in and out of numerous foster homes after my mom's murder, then surviving on skid row in my teens and early twenties, I had forged a complicated, lone wolf persona and allowed few people through that. I knew Matt was only trying to comfort me. My partner is a good investigator, and I trusted him with my life. But his compassion wasn't capable of healing my wounds.

A spasm rolled from my shoulders down to my toes. I swore I'd just felt Dee's palm massaging the skin of my back.

"Relax," she'd said. "Okay. Here comes the sting."

The tea kettle on the stove whistled. The concentrated steam briefly lifted my bitter mood from the realization that a personal expression Dee-Dee had started would never be finished. I filled the mug up to the brim and left the green tea to steep.

I barged through the French doors and crossed the living room to my computer desk, situated against the brick wall by the window. The soles of my wet riding boots squeaked on the hardwood floor. I needed to find an old address book that contained info on Dee-Dee's family in San Francisco.

Being a self-admitted slob didn't make the search easy. I plopped down in the plush high-back chair, then proceeded to shift assorted items and knick-knacks around, knocking over a tall energy drink can in the process. I grabbed the can, tipped it upright, then tossed it into the trash. I covered the flat, yellowish spill with wads of tissue.

My eye caught on a picture of Dee-Dee and me at Lollapalooza '93, cheering, our arms draped over each other's shoulders.

After that, corporate America had sunk its commercial claws into the grunge lifestyle.

Taunted by memories and lost choices, I grabbed the frame and slapped it face down, hard enough that I heard the glass pane crack.

I retreated to the kitchen and rummaged through a junk drawer, sliding a crumpled, coffee-stained crossword puzzle book aside to uncover a fifth of Jack Daniels I remembered splashing on Matt's shoulder to clean a gunshot wound years ago. I paused, absently rubbing my lips, then slammed the drawer shut before the booze could lull my alcoholism into surrendering to just one drink. I picked up the mug from the bar and took a gulp, grimaced, and dumped the lukewarm tea in the kitchen sink.

Feeling my hands begin to shake from either adrenaline or shock, I grabbed my car keys off the hook by the door, locked my loft, and jogged down the stairs. My pounding feet probably woke up my neighbors, but I didn't really give a shit. The burned-out lights in the courtyard main entrance didn't slow me down. The red glow from a hunter's moon illuminated the walkway. A stiff breeze rustled the shrubs lining both sides and whipped strands of my thick hair around my face. I disarmed my Saturn's alarm, yanked the door open, and plopped down behind the wheel to crank the engine to life.

"Shut the hell up," I told the shorted out *Check Engine* light; it stopped beeping and blinking as I peeled out from the curb.

A couple blocks uphill, I turned left off Irving. Revving up to just above forty, I steered with one hand and fastened my safety belt with the other; the shoulder strap locked, squeezing the wind out of me for a few seconds, when I stomped the brake at the intersection. The staggering transient using a shopping cart for a walker was oblivious. I flashed the brights at her. She walked slower. While I waited, I snatched up a mix

CD and shoved it into the stereo. The driving beat of Iggy Pop's "Lust For Life" tuned up my pulse.

I spot-checked for oncoming vehicles. Seeing headlights approaching fast, I whipped left onto Burnside Avenue and sped eastward. When the light at Powell's Books switched to yellow, I breezed through it at fifty. Traffic at Broadway began to thicken. I wove around cruisers and assholes.

I zipped across the Burnside Bridge. I needed to make a left onto Grand Avenue, but the *Left Turn Prohibited* sign swinging in the wind above the intersection gave me pause. Though following the rules of the road was the last thing on my mind, I didn't want to fuck up any motorists to get where I was going. So I powered up a block and took a detour around like a good little Portlander. As I took the exit for I-84 East, fat raindrops splattered the windshield.

A driver in front of me took forever merging into sparse traffic. I leaned on my horn and flashed the brights. "What do you need?" I yelled. "An invitation?" I checked the right lane to ensure it was clear and left the PT Cruiser in a spray of mist.

When I passed the Hollywood District the sheets of rain pounding the top of my car sounded like buckets of nails. I switched the wipers on. Other vehicles, white oncoming headlights, and red brake lights blended like melting steel and wax. Squinting, I kept the road reflectors in focus.

The left lane seemed empty. I swerved there to go seventy and climbed up to seventy-five. Sleater-Kinney's "The Drama You've Been Craving" was track two.

"A little rainfall," I said, addressing the other motorists, "and you pussies drive like tourists."

I could still smell the aroma of the joint Dee had smoked at a rest stop on the drive back from the coast. Her spinal injury allowed her a medical marijuana prescription. Cracking my window to vent the odor, I grinned at the memory of her lips pursed to suck in a long toke, and my own numbing euphoria, stoned on Dee's homegrown weed. I'd sustained a contact high in our motel room, where the bittersweet scent had drifted out the balcony screen door, which Dee had insisted on leaving open so the pounding of the surf could relieve our tensions. The Mary Jane had still given me the customary junk food cravings.

Every muscle in my body coiled as red lights rushed toward the Saturn's windshield. "Shit!" I almost mashed the brake pedal, a knee-jerk response that could've led to hydroplaning into an uncontrollable skid.

Spotting the sign reminding me the I-205 exit was a quarter mile away, I flashed a look into the rearview mirror and double-checked a blind spot. Cars were moving up, but their speeds weren't high enough to stop me swerving into the left lane between two semis. The trucker behind me leaned on his horn, but decelerated to give me space. Once we cleared the curve of the exit onto 205 South, I moved to the far right, and propelled the Saturn at seventy-five again.

"Where the hell are you going anyway, you crazy bitch?" I asked myself. I didn't know, really. I needed to drive fast and evade my feelings.

"This is going to be my masterpiece," Dee had told me, the intense pride in her voice washing over me like a first-time experience. Her tone dropped. "When we take a break, I need to talk to you about another matter."

"Ooh, that doesn't sound like your average girl talk," I'd said casually, my mind wrapped in endorphins.

Dee had paused to take a long, deep breath that told me whatever the topic was, it really pissed her off. "I might need to hire you for a case."

We never took that break, though. Maybe we were too stoned. Maybe our brief vacation together had helped Dee work through what'd upset her so much.

No.

Dee was killed for the job she'd forgotten to hire me for.

I leered at myself in the rearview mirror. "You're so self-fucking-centered," I screamed, banging the steering wheel with a fist.

I hung a sharp right on Highway 224 at the fruit stand before the Mount Hood exit. Beyond that point I gave my reflexes a lethal workout that would've made Dale Earnhardt Jr. turn white. I tore through the country backroads at speeds in excess of seventy-five, an ideal course of evasive maneuvers to purge my guilt.

Three

Matt Grudge

THE SECOND hand on the round plastic clock above my office door ticked around ten past midnight. Leslie and I had started at 7:00 a.m. yesterday and caffeinated or not, I felt the distance to the wall closing. I still hadn't heard back from the information sources I'd e-mailed and telephoned. Slapping the laptop closed, I pushed away from my desk and slouched down in the swivel chair, whipped.

Taking my mug and the pot into the compact bathroom off the foyer between our spaces, I dumped the remaining coffee down the drain. The plumbing gurgled. I lumbered out to Leslie's office to put them away, and picked up my backpack from the couch in the small waiting area out in front of her desk.

I returned to the bathroom and dropped the sack on the toilet seat. Unzipping one of the side pouches, I removed my toothbrush and a travel-size tube of toothpaste. I took my T-shirt off and tossed it on the backpack, then brushed furiously at the coffee stains on my teeth. Globs of pasty spittle plopped into the sink and spattered my chest, which I wiped off with a washcloth. I may have been messy with my hygiene, but at least my dentist appreciated it; so did my health insurance deductible.

The loop recently pierced through my left nipple looked a little red, but wasn't itching or burning. I soaked a cotton ball with rubbing alcohol anyway and waylaid a possible infection. I bit my lip at the sting and told myself to man up, my eyes on my left biceps, where thorns wrapped an alert eye. It was the first tattoo I'd ever gotten, an extreme variation on the Pinkerton *We Never Sleep* logo. I thought about the artist who'd given it to me, and wondered if she still worked at Femme Ink.

While I was at it, I peered at the other piercings in my face. The blue zircon studs and surgical steel loops in my earlobes looked fine. The gold loop in the outer corner of my left eyebrow had a crooked hair growing through it that I plucked with tweezers. Splashing water on my face, I patted it dry with a towel, then left the bathroom to make sure the outer door was locked.

I remembered my cell phone needed recharging. As I reached inside the damp jacket that I'd hung on the row of hooks by the door, the phone vibrated. I flipped it open. Pepper Rourke, the tattoo artist I'd just been reminiscing about, had sent me a text: *Saw U outside while detectives interviewed me. CSI finally gone. I'm in the apartment upstairs. Can't be alone. Please come over. - P*

Pulling on a tan cotton T-shirt and a brown corduroy shirt over that, I shrugged at my holey jeans, closed my rucksack and slung it over my shoulder, and grabbed my coat. I locked up on the way out.

On the corner across from Pioneer Place, I debated getting my car from the lot a couple of blocks away where a steep fee reserved a pair of spaces. Looking up and down the canyon of concrete and glass as a street washer rolled up the boulevard, I breathed in the crisp air. The night lights twinkled a little brighter after the earlier rainstorm. The swirling patches of gray overhead could've delivered another downpour at any time, but that didn't faze an Oregonian as much as the rising gasoline prices.

The blue and teal reflection of the downtown cityscape rippled in the water around me as I hiked across the Morrison Bridge. The cardio helped to purge my anger and frustration at Leslie pushing me away. We'd seen each other through a number of situations that'd made cases personal in the last fifteen years. What had caused her to lose faith in me now?

I paused at the corner of the flower shop next to Bob's barbershop. A lime green Honda Civic zoomed west through a red light at the intersection of Grand and Morrison, subwoofer pounding out hip-hop bass. The diner across the street a block down from Femme Ink had closed hours ago, but the neon *Open* sign had been left on. It flickered and hummed.

The only spot on the block brighter than the streetlights was the window above the tattoo parlor. The beacon of loneliness and sleeplessness pulled at my sense of purpose. If my own partner couldn't find solace in our partnership, then maybe I could be a sounding board for a potential person of interest in Dee-Dee's murder.

I jogged against the light. A massive flash of lightning strobed over the Weatherly Building, throwing my shadow on the dumpster near the fire escape. I tugged the trash receptacle a few feet closer and clambered on top of it to pull the bottom ladder down.

As I ascended the rungs, rain came down in a showering drizzle. I knelt down on the third floor platform, the cold grating stamping my bare kneecap. The windowpane squeaked as I wiped beads of water off the glass to peer inside at the hallway of a kitchenette and oak dining nook. It all looked cozy and inviting. Steam rose from a large cast-iron saucepan on the range; I felt some of it seeping through the bottom of the window, which was cracked open. The aroma of garlic, onion, coriander, and cumin teased my nostrils. I'd skipped dinner and my stomach growled. Moby's "Porcelain" whispered from the beat-up portable radio that sat on the booth table where a game of solitaire was laid out.

Still as a gothic gargoyle keeping sentinel, I peered through the parted blinds to make a positive ID. "Pepper, is that really you?" I muttered to myself through chapped lips as, feet snug in Garfield slippers, the scrawny, granola-type chick from my past entered the kitchen hip-walking on toned hiker's legs. She wore tan hemp capris and a too-tight, black and yellow *Keep Portland Weird!* tank over muscular curves. No bra. The firm, high C-cups on her bombshell figure didn't need the support.

Fifteen years ago, as an aloof seventeen-year-old, she'd confided in her filthy-rich foster family that she wished to pursue an art degree instead of a law degree to ultimately become a tattoo artist. The assholes emptied the joint savings account where Pepper had socked away a small fortune for college tuition.

Abandoned, kicked to the street, unable to complete high school to graduate, Pepper met Dee-Dee at a farmer's market in Seven Corners. The tattoo aficionado took notice of the elegant, unique script the rangy hippie nymph was drawing on a billboard to promote fresh fruit. They hit it off.

Dee-Dee boarded Pepper, put her to work as a receptionist in Femme Ink, financed her art education, then mentored Pepper in the tattoo discipline. One year of prosperity later, Pepper looked me up because my PI practice metamorphosed from researching white collar crimes for suits to locating missing teens in skid row environs. Leslie and I dug up what her foster parents had done with Pepper's money. We'd waived over half of our fee and expenses, and Pepper gave us tattoos to make up the difference.

Pepper opened the compact fridge across from the dining nook by the window. I saw her fingernails were painted a glittering purple. My favorite color. The chilled air hardened her nipples into perky eraser tips.

I wondered if our fuck buddy fling the month after she'd tattooed me would pose a problem. Our budding careers had fizzled it out. The passion for my life's work now stronger than ever, I intended to keep that awkward history swept under the rug.

I tapped the window with my fingertip.

Pepper jumped and dropped a plastic bag of leafy greens, her shoulder-length, fine chestnut hair with strawberry red highlights twirling as she spun toward the window. Behind black horn-rimmed glasses, sullen, coffee-colored eyes widened with fright. The frames were positioned slightly askew on her pert nose and the lenses made her irises sparkle like precious stones.

"Jesus," she gasped, placing a hand over her chest as she backed against the refrigerator door; it knocked a few bottles and jars loose to hit the linoleum. "Matt, you *dumb* ass."

Pulling aside the shades, she pushed the window up. When one side jammed at a crooked angle in the track, her yoga-toned muscles compensated. Rather than stare at the sculpted lines of her abs straining against the stubborn wood, I grabbed the other side of the frame to help wiggle it free.

"Watch your nails," I said.

Once the window was open all the way, she pulled on my damp shoulder as I lifted a leg over the sill to climb through. "You have something against using the front or back door?" she asked.

I unslung my rucksack to drop it on the floor by the booth. "Hazard of my profession," I told her. "The direct approach seldom leads to where I want to go."

"I'm happy you came," she said with a sniffle, wrapping long arms around my neck for a lingering hug. Black flames licked up the sleeves tattooed on those alabaster arms, the skin stippled by freckles that I knew covered her entire body.

"It was horrible, Matt. I returned from picking up some groceries and found Dee in her office, slumped over her drafting table. The last couple of days were really jammed up for her, and I thought she'd fallen asleep from exhaustion. When I nudged her to wake up, she fell off the stool. Blood collected in the pencil holder dribbled . . ."

"Shhh," I said, rubbing her back. I walked her backward a few steps. "Don't think about that now. Sit down." I guided her trembling body inside the nook, gently unfolded her arms from around me, then snatched a napkin out of the ornate wooden holder on the table and offered it to her.

Pepper dabbed at the redness around her eyes. "Thanks," she said.

The teapot whistled. I found it behind the soup on the stove and filled a mug already prepared, then returned it to the burner, which I switched off. The aroma of chamomile wafted with the steam to fill the intimate space with calm. While the tea steeped, I shifted over to the sink to wash and dry my hands.

I turned around to see Pepper shaking. She tossed the wadded up napkin at the trashcan a short distance from the window and missed. She made to get up, reaching for the serrated knife on the counter between the fridge and the stove.

I snatched the handle away. "No, no. Sit your pretty ass back down," I said, bending down to retrieve the bag of greens I'd made her drop. "You can just delegate."

A partial grin accentuated the beauty mark on her lower left cheek near the corner of her mouth. Her eyes sparked with annoyance. "I'm a big girl now," she said. "I can make my own supper."

I rinsed the kale under cold water for a minute, shook it dry, then placed the greens on a cutting board I slid out of the counter. "No doubt," I said, pointing the tip of the knife at her. "But you're in too much shock right now to hold a blade steady. And a tattoo artist with damaged hands isn't going to have much of a livelihood."

"Since you put it that way," Pepper said, pouting a little, "chop up the kale and stir it into the pan. Give me my tea first, though."

I began opening and closing the cupboard doors above the counter and the stove.

"I don't need a saucer," she told me.

I found a short stack of them—square and round hand-sculpted ceramics of assorted colors worthy of coming from Saturday Market. I grabbed a round blue one that didn't have any cracks and set it and the mug down near her solitaire game. "As my grandpa used to say when he prepared a homemade meal," I said, "presentation is everything."

"You're sweet."

I gave her a wink, then started opening and closing drawers to find the utensils. The one under the cupboard of plates, bowls, and saucers was loaded with plastic baggies, a roll of small garbage bags, and plastic zip ties. The next one back was a junk drawer. I marked the miniature flashlight for later. I opened the third drawer over. "There you are," I said, and grabbed a spoon.

I handed it to Pepper, my gaze pausing on the polished steel bracelet that adorned her right wrist.

"Thank you. There's a plastic bowl of sliced lemons in the fridge," Pepper said, gesturing with the cards in her hand at the icebox door decorated with magnets and stickers bearing the logos for local indie rock and punk bands. I got the small container out and placed it on the table.

She squished the tea bag against the spoon, rested it on the saucer, then squeezed a lemon wedge over the chamomile tea. She sucked on the pulpy rind, then gave me a mischievous grin when she caught me watching her. I wanted to taste that citrus tang on her lips, and she knew it. Clearing her throat, she nodded at the stove.

"Yeah," I said.

As Pepper searched the correct row to lay down a seven of clubs, I chopped up the kale, with the hard spine removed.

"So," Pepper said, "I take it you're still a private detective. Do you spy on a lot of cheating spouses through cheap hotel windows from fire escapes?"

"No," I said with a chuckle. "Leslie and I try to avoid infidelity work."

"It's good to know you're still partners. That time Leslie brought you by for your first tat, I thought you had as much potential of blending into the punk underworld as a cop at Lollapalooza."

"I don't know about that," I said, finding a rhythm with the edge of the blade and the cutting board. *Chop chop chop chop chop.* "There are plenty of detectives nowadays who are chameleons undercover."

"You're the first law enforcement type I ever met who had the guts to get a tattoo," Pepper told me. "And now look at you. You dye your hair blond all the time; who'd know you're really reddish-brown? You keep in better shape—lean and ripped without looking like a steroid junky. You're even starting to get a little weathered around the eyes, my favorite part in a man: that experienced look."

The knife slipped and I cut my finger. "*Ouch!* Fuck. Thanks. I'm not so sure about the experienced part, though." Before I could bleed on Pepper's food, I tossed the knife on the counter and moved to the sink to run cold water over the finger.

She dropped the cards on the checker-tiled floor and jumped up out of the booth. "I'll get you a Band-Aid." She rushed out of the kitchen.

While I wrapped the cut up, Pepper scooped up the kale with her hands and added it to the saucepan. I moved to the fridge to fetch a filtered pitcher of ice water I'd seen there, filled a glass I grabbed from the strainer next to the sink, and took a seat in the nook. As Pepper opened a can of white beans, rinsed them, then stirred them into the saucepan, I picked up the red Bicycle cards she'd dropped. I bunched them together with a rubber band I plucked from the clean ashtray in the middle of the table and tossed the deck over by the radio. It was playing Sarah McLachlan's soothing "Angel."

Pepper plopped down on the seat across from me and blew a few locks of hair out of her eyes in an expression of exhaustion.

Dark crescents sagged under eyes still red from tears. "Dinner will be ready in about thirty minutes," she said.

"Smells good. What is it?"

"Kale and white bean soup," she told me. "A recipe I picked up while backpacking through Europe."

Interest rising, I leaned forward. "Which part?"

"Romania."

"I bet the landscapes made for breathless hiking," I said before lifting my glass for a drink of water.

"The summer heat did that," Pepper reflected. "Temperatures always hovered in the low nineties."

"Summer of . . . ?"

"It was '94 or '95," she said. "A vacation Dee paid for after I managed Femme Ink a whole year solo, while she was opening another shop elsewhere. She also wanted the trip to expand my artistic palette." Getting weepy again, she grabbed a fresh napkin to blow her nose. With the silver loops in her septum and right nostril, she blew delicately.

"What designs are popular there?" I asked.

"Same art you'll find all over the world, really," Pepper said. "The tattooists I hooked up with broadened my skills in perspective, color. Please tell me you weren't expecting a *60 Minutes* monologue about tags on slaves, human trafficking."

Actually, I was recollecting silently that the summer of '94 or '95 may have followed the deterioration of our affair. Maybe Pepper had taken it harder than I thought. I shrugged off the brief narcissism and focused on my job: fighting crime. "We both know Russian mobs use tats to show rank."

Pepper chuckled. "The most criminal scenario I heard about was an artist being sued for inking sixty stars on a client's face, when she'd supposedly wanted only six."

"Was the girl drunk?"

"No," she said, her tone passionate. "The artists there are almost militant with their tattoo regulations. The customer isn't allowed to drink while getting tattooed, and if they're too intoxicated entering the parlor, their business is turned away. What really happened was, a young woman wanted to rebel one last time on the eve of her marriage and when her parents and fiancé saw what happened, they went straight after the tattooist and accused him of drugging or hypnotizing the girl. Just what inkers don't need."

"Like the hepatitis scare in New York City, '61," I said.

"Right."

Pushing up from the table, Pepper moved to the stove and ladled generous portions of the stew into bowls. Adding a wooden soup spoon to each, she brought them to the table and snuggled into the booth, folding her legs up on the seat. Bowing her head over her bowl, she inhaled the aromatic steam that climbed up her glasses as fog.

I shoveled a heaping spoonful of the hearty concoction into my mouth and chewed appreciatively; the vegetables were tender, the hot broth warming. "Delicious."

Pepper's lips tipped in a faint smile before she puckered them to blow on her first spoonful.

We sipped and slurped without any conversation for a while. The pain of losing her friend and employer seemed a little numbed, and the fifteen-year gap since our fast relationship was being rekindled in the bleak silence between survivors; we were both that and, deep down, idealists.

"Remember what we ate that first night we spent together, Matt?"

"Nothing this satisfying," I lied.

After challenging me with a smoldering glare, Pepper slipped out of the nook and tidied up, ladling the leftover stew into a tall plastic container and rinsing the dishes before drying her hands on the dish towel hanging from the oven handle. I took in the line of her back, curving around the swell of her hips, then her tight ass shaped by miles of walking.

"I'm going to get ready for bed," she said. "Would you mind staying the night? The crime scene technicians and detective couldn't figure out how the killer got inside."

I rose and stepped over to the sink to wash my bowl and spoon. During the light meal, I'd read Pepper as being more than upset, and now I knew why. She was scared. "Just show me the couch," I said.

With a sweet smile, Pepper tenderly caressed my cheek, then turned to lead me through the foyer that linked the kitchen with the bedroom to the right and a door on the left I presumed led to the storeroom floor above the tattoo parlor.

What the small dwelling lacked in size (it wasn't much bigger than a Motel 6 room), it made up for with decor. Aside from the usual amenities of a full-sized bed, side table, dresser, and entertainment stand with a TV/DVD combo set caked with dust, the studio walls featured an oil painting of San Francisco at night, a bamboo shelf holding assorted shot glasses, the cartoon rendering of a 1920s water carnival at Coney Island, and sitting next to a clock radio on the nightstand, a round, cobalt blue tobacco jar from which emanated the scent of incense. Dim light from a banker's lamp on the dresser stretched shadows.

A door behind me shut hard, spinning me around. From the sound of running water, I presumed Pepper had gone into the washroom to brush her teeth. I moved to the door in the far left corner at the foot of the bed, my leg brushing a red and orange afghan quilt. The door was tight; I tugged it open to see a walk-in closet. A folding bed was tucked away in the corner behind a stack of packing boxes and a splintered baseball bat. No pillow. I glanced back at the head of the bed to see only one there.

"Pepper," I called out, "if there's a linen closet or cupboard underneath the sink, can you see if there's a—" I stopped, ogling her topless reflection in the window.

I turned around. The warmth in my groin that'd been gradually building since watching her through the apartment window ignited into a blaze.

She walked toward me. Her fingertips hooked the waistband of the blue lacy panties and she effortlessly shed the skin-tight undergarment one inch at a time. She kicked the glossy fabric between my legs, then faced me toe to toe. I inhaled the mint and alcohol from the toothpaste and mouthwash on her breath.

I didn't get a chance to admire the new tats on her body. Gentle hands reached up and pulled the corduroy shirt down from my shoulders. Bunching up my T-shirt, Pepper pressed the smooth swells of her breasts up against my chest. I felt my penis enlarge.

She fingered the tattoo on my biceps that she'd inked so many years ago. "The color's bleached. I'll touch it up later."

The gaze she held on me, augmented through her eyeglasses, was hypnotic. Her fingertips trailed down my arm, then lifted my hand to place my palm on her breast.

"This might be crossing—"

She put her index finger against my lips and wrapped her other hand around my belt to jerk me forward. Both her hands dropped to unclasp the buckle, and she yanked the faux leather free of the belt loops and tossed it aside. I finished pulling my shirt off. She led me around and pushed me back onto the bed, immediately crawling up to straddle my thighs. The box springs squeaked.

Pepper sucked on my abs just above my navel, hard enough to leave a hickey. Then she ran the tip of her tongue up my torso. My pecs twitched. Her teeth pulled gently at the hoop in my nipple, while her fingers unfastened my jeans and yanked the zipper apart. My inked cock sprang out.

"Holy shit! After we're done fucking, you've gotta tell me about this tat."

Before I could say no, I was groaning with pleasure. My dick throbbed as Pepper stroked me with a fist, then moved her face down to my crotch as drops of pre-cum trickled out. I felt the round, metallic surface of a stud roll around the skin of my head, before the moist tip of her tongue lapped at my juices.

I could burst at any minute. Yearning to release inside her, together, I was about to warn her not to take me into her mouth all the way when, as if reading my mind, Pepper smothered my mouth with a long kiss. The ceiling fan above the bed spun on low. It chilled our sizzling bodies and reverberated our moans around the room.

The tongue massage paused for us to snatch a few breaths. I was blasted from arousal. Her lips moved in to make out again. Clutching her waist, I spun Pepper around to get on top. The sudden movement flipped her hair in a luxuriant wave. Her eyeglasses almost flew off. She yelped with excitement.

I removed the last of my clothing. My dick grew stiffer. I focused on my breathing to sustain how long I could last.

I slid down against silky-smooth skin slick with sweat to Pepper's crotch. I gave her Brazilian-waxed pubes a poke with my tongue, then hooked one of her long legs over my shoulder. The bottom of her other foot whispered across the bed as she spread her other leg. This unfurled her moist pussy like a *Penthouse* centerfold's. I teased the length of her labia minora, caressing the long, succulent lips that peeked out with the tip of my nose.

She giggled. Her scent of mangoes and lemons made me salivate. I licked her clit the way a dehydrated animal laps up spring water. Pepper's fingertips massaged the back of my head.

"Oh shit, baby," she said, the tempo of her voice racing to catch up with gasps coming in rapid succession. "You found my spot quick this time."

I put my neck into the up and down, round and round motions with my tongue, listening as her moans rose to a fever pitch, then panting screams.

"Ooh Matt your tongue, keep moving your tongue just like that—feels sooo good—unhh . . ." A sigh of ecstasy trickled from her glistening lips.

"Hope you're ready for more where that came from," she said as her powerful legs hooked my thighs to pull me upward. A tiny wiggle of her hips pulled my swollen cock inside her. Bucking up hard, she squeezed her pelvic muscles—squeeze, hold, then release—longer and harder with each thrust. I'd never felt so stimulated.

"Fill me up, honey," Pepper breathed into my ear.

Rolling us over to get on top, she ground her hips against me to sustain my ejaculation.

Her back arched in orgasm. "Jeez, you're huge," she shrieked. "Unhh, ooh, nnnh, uhh—"

I felt her vaginal muscles tighten as she came, and pumped faster, grunting with pleasure at the pressure. I fired my glutes for more penetration.

Squeeze, three-second hold, release. Squeeze, four-second hold, biting and sucking my nipple ring, release. "You like that, huh, Matt. 'Cause you're—unhh—*throbbing* on my clit—*yes!* YES! YEAH—I'M—nnnh, uhh—COMING!" Squeeze, five-second hold to French kiss, release. Squeeze, five-second hold . . .

"Ooh, uhh, uhh—OH GOD! I want it, Matt! Come! COME! *Oooh!*"

An animal growl exploded through my lips as I exploded.

Absorbing spasms from my release, Pepper collapsed forward, probably to cuddle, then stopped, bracing her hands on my chest. A bead of sweat trickled down one lens of her glasses.

"Goodness, you're still hard," she said amorously.

The appetite in her voice made my heart race. Pepper clutched my biceps to roll us back over, then clamped her calves across the tops of my thighs to piston me into her even deeper.

●

RAIN BEAT the window like pennies poured into a mason jar. The white noise lulled me into a few hours of sleep, spooned around Pepper. My hand rested on the soft skin just underneath her right breast. Our breathing was relaxed, tension free.

I woke with a start.

Once my vision adjusted to the dark, I pushed up on my elbow to study Pepper in slumber. Her mouth was curved up in a contented grin. I gently pulled my hand off her. She didn't stir. Lifting the covers, I slid out of the bed. I hunted up the clothes that'd been tossed around the room and dressed, and pulled on my sneakers without bothering to tie the laces.

In the kitchen I went to the junk drawer for the miniature flashlight, then moved to the door on the left in the foyer that separated the kitchen and bedroom. I unbolted the door, unfastened the chain, and opened it slowly. The hinges didn't make a sound. I twisted the flashlight on and followed its thin beam down the stairs to the next landing and a door that bore a hand-drawn sign with red and violet bubble letters spelling *Storage*. I paused, identifying faint noises as natural settling within the walls before opening the door. I found what I needed on a short stack of plastic totes: an open box of latex gloves. I snapped a pair on and returned to the landing.

I continued down the next flight of stairs to the rear entrance to the parlor, startling when the step third from the bottom creaked like a coffin lid being pried open. Recovering quickly, I proceeded into Femme Ink.

For years, it was an urban oasis for tattoo enthusiasts wanting to personalize their alternative lifestyles. Yesterday afternoon it was a crime scene. Now, it felt like a tomb cold with death. Chills made my flesh clammy. The latex gloves filled up with sweat faster than usual.

The wide back hall was decorated with clipped pictures arranged into massive collages. I spotted a few celebrities. I stopped at a sun-bleached Polaroid of Leslie and Dee-Dee. My partner looked young and carefree, twenty-one or twenty-three maybe. Her head was tilted back in laughter as Dee-Dee, an empty tequila shooter in her hand, licked course margarita salt off of her neck.

Shit. I gulped. I hadn't known their friendship went that far back. That intimacy explained Leslie's shrouded, silent feelings. A cocktail of vengeance was brewing inside her, I realized.

I smirked at a collage labeled *Virgin Tats*. There, off center, was a snapshot of Pepper giving me my first ink. Free of the stiff security firm I'd worked for, I'd finally let my hair grow, and sported a reddish-brown mullet in the photo, with not a speck of gray in it. My roman-collared shirt was unbuttoned, so I was able to breathe deeply through the stinging pain.

A reflection in the mirror at the first artist station from the rear hallway caught my eye. There were traces of gray above my ears now, visible in my blond crew cut. I sighed and moved into the parlor's main area, panning the light back and forth at my feet. I didn't want to upset any evidence the police may have missed that might help me.

The largest work space was on the other side of the room, just to the left of a reception desk, and underneath a huge, full-color portrait of Dee-Dee from the thighs up signed *Cooney*. I headed toward it, then froze in my tracks. Every inch of the lounge chair, drafting table, and desk shelves loaded with memorabilia was dusted with fingerprint powder. I was allergic to the shit.

My sinuses flared up. I covered my nose and backed up to the crescent-shaped check-in desk to snag a Kleenex. I hacked into it. When the coughing attack subsided, I wadded the tissue up to stuff it in my back pocket, then grabbed a few fresh ones to cover my nose and mouth.

I pulled my cell phone out of my pocket and moved toward Dee-Dee's tattooing area again. I opened the camera app, then cursed when the low battery indicator blinked. I'd forgotten the damn thing needed charging. I managed to snap five pictures from assorted angles close up before the display went blank.

The lights popped on overhead.

"Oh, fuck," I said, then whirled around.

The baseball bat lowered and Pepper's shoulders relaxed. "What the hell are you doing down here?" she yelled.

She had on a pair of green Oregon Ducks sweatpants and a yellow, sweat-soaked camisole. I noted how tight her fists still choked the bat and took a few seconds to pick my words just right. Then I figured there was no such thing, because I'd just been inside her.

"Looking at where Dee-Dee was murdered," I said.

Pepper smacked the top of the reception desk with the bat. "You could've just asked me. Is this the real reason you accepted my invitation? Did you think you could just fuck me to sleep then snoop through my life?"

I dropped the flashlight to hold my hands up, palms out in surrender. "No."

"Don't lie to me, you asshole," she shouted louder, raising the bat.

Flinching, I raised my arms up to absorb a blow. "Pepper, listen. I was doing my job, for chrissakes."

Pepper dropped the slugger. It bounced a couple times on the linoleum floor. She yanked a set of keys from a hot pink bracelet on her wrist, then stomped over to the front entrance. Unlocking the door, she yanked it open. "Out."

At the threshold I paused to look Pepper in the face. "I didn't mean to hurt you."

She drove a knee into my crotch. I grabbed my balls and bent forward, groaning in agony.

"Multiply that by X," Pepper said, "and that's how I *feel* right now, Matthew." Stepping around me, she kicked me in the side.

Off balance, I tumbled out onto the sidewalk, the side of my face splashing into a puddle. At least the rain had stopped. By the time the pain between my legs subsided enough for me to stand up, my rucksack had landed in the street. Making sure no vehicles were approaching, I stumbled out to grab my stuff.

I peered at the B of A ATM machine across the street from Femme Ink before returning to the sidewalk. I set the bag on a newspaper kiosk, massaged my groin, then pulled the latex gloves off and tossed them in a trashcan next to the phone booth near the diner.

The rucksack slung over my shoulder, I limped back across the bridge to the office.

The hard drive woke when I opened the laptop screen. I sent a brief e-mail to a particular security guard at the bank, requesting a copy of the ATM security camera footage from yesterday. My one-armed friend wouldn't have gotten the job without listing me as a reference.

I dozed for a few hours before the laptop pinged a new mail alert. The Gulf War vet agreed to my favor. All I had to do was buy him lunch.

FOUR

Leslie Crow

EARLY MORNING rousted me out of my sweaty, uncomfortable sleep with sunlight and chirping birds. I turned my face away, eyes clenched, intent on absorbing the last of a dream in which I was attending the execution of Dee's killer.

The drapes separating the witness box from the sterile medical chamber whispered apart to reveal *me* strapped to the lethal injection table.

"Nuh-uh . . ." Drool slid down the side of my chin with a groggy murmur.

I squirmed, feeling my skin pinch and the bite of the IV needle being inserted into my trembling arm.

A solid thump against the windshield brought me bolt upright in the reclined car seat. Unclasping the glove box, I punched the combo on the portable gun safe. The lid hissed open and I jammed my hand inside to grasp the Glock.

I paused to catch my breath, then rolled my eyes.

"Sorry," a teenage boy said, waggling a Frisbee, "my bad."

"Yeah, yeah," I said, "okay." Shooing him away with my other hand, I released the pistol, then pushed the safe door shut until I heard the click telling me the handgun was secure. He jogged away to rejoin his friends, and gave the bright orange disc a wrist flick.

"You little shit," I said, wiping the spittle off my face.

The stereo clock indicated the time was a little past 9:00 a.m. I raised the seat back to an upright position and watched the group of teens hurling the Frisbee to one another. Tracking the disc's motion helped to wake me up until a decent cup of coffee would come around. Sleeping in the car all night made me stiff. Leading with my chin, I rotated my head through a range-of-motion stretch to loosen my rear neck and shoulder muscles.

Where had my reckless driving excursion ended, anyway? I spotted a restroom building, some covered picnic tables, and a hill studded with trees whose leaves were turning gold and red. I watched the teenagers traipse around with discs of assorted colors in their hands, then powered my window down and listened. Off in the distance I could make out the roar of a river. I didn't hear engines from any traffic nearby. So that ruled out this being a rest stop. It had to be a park somewhere.

I dug inside the side pocket of my black jeans for my iPhone. Tapping the map app icon, I checked my current location: Milo McIver State Park, four miles west of Estacada.

Reaching behind the passenger seat for my black tactical go-bag, I slung the nylon strap over my shoulder and headed for the women's room. The *Out of Order* sign made me turn around and check the men's. All of the stalls were empty. I set the go-bag on the sink closest to the door. Unzipping the blue hoodie that'd kept me warm, I pulled it off, then the ragged black tee emblazoned with the faded logo of a local metal band, and scrunched both into the bag's main compartment. I withdrew a fresh sports bra and a beige long-sleeved tee with a sweetheart neckline before unfastening the push-up bra I'd worn yesterday and tossing that into the bag as well. I pulled on the fresh bra. The hoops pierced through my nipples made indentations in the material. I rolled on some deodorant, pulled the T-shirt on, then ran a brush through my shoulder-length hair.

Closing my go-bag, I slung it back over my shoulder and returned to the Saturn. On my way there, I double-checked Dee's private address and got directions there from my current location with my iPhone. She'd kept an apartment above Femme Ink and a condo in the Pearl, but a close relative had willed her a horse ranch, a calm oasis she maintained to take breaks from urban life and to grow her pot. The Google map placed it closer to my current location than Estacada.

I knew where Dee kept the spare key hidden. Maybe I could find her family's unlisted San Francisco address in that house.

I walked around my car, looking for any fresh dents or scratches. It needed a wash. The left rear tire was missing a hubcap. I popped the trunk open with a key fob double-tap, tossed my go-bag down next to a small plastic crate that contained some roadside emergency gear, and smacked the trunk shut. Sliding behind the wheel, I warmed up the Saturn until the windows defrosted, and took off.

In Carver, an independent community of Damascus, I pulled into a drive-thru espresso shack and waited while the barista prepared my latte with a machine that wheezed like a sick animal. I peered at the cafe across the highway. The family-owned joint had gained a little notoriety recently by being a shooting location for a teen angst vampire movie.

Hot, double-cupped drink in hand, I waited for a dozen vehicles before I pulled out into traffic behind a cherry red jeep with a temporary license taped inside the rear window. The rig must've been new for the driver, because it was moving really slow. I didn't mind, though. It gave me time to savor the robust flavor of my coffee: Stumptown's Hairbender blend.

I switched the stereo on and turned the blasting volume down, then switched it from CD to a local station just in time for a news break. Nothing was mentioned about Dee's death, or an investigation. There was a brief announcement about Mayor Sam Adams and Governor John Kitzhaber attending a black tie dinner tonight with dignitaries of the Russian embassy from San Francisco. The location for the event was withheld.

I gulped down the last of my java just on the other side of the first bend in the Carver Curves, a treacherous stretch of road that winds through a forest corridor alongside the Clackamas River. The fall colors on the trees belonged in an Impressionist painting. Dried leaves peppered the windshield. A roadside memorial composed of wooden crosses, pictures, and flowers reminded me that although the serpentine road made for a pretty, scenic drive, it killed people. Chucking the empty cup in the back, I placed both hands on the wheel. I spotted a set of fresh skid marks near a gap in the guardrail and wondered if I'd made them last night.

"*Jesus Christ!*" I shouted as a huge semi towing a massive pile of logs came barreling around a corner, its turn wide on the incline. I jerked the wheel. Increasing speed, I used the gaping entrance to a gravel utility road to avoid collision. Some of my latte tried to come back up.

Breathing deeply, I exited the curves. I took my right hand off the wheel and held it up, trying to hold it steady. It trembled with the last of an adrenaline surge. I chuckled and gave it a shake. "Yeesh."

A mile up the road I passed a general store, then one hundred yards beyond that, I pulled into the drive for Dee's horse ranch. The potholes in the unpaved path jostled the Saturn's suspension. I needed a bigger vehicle, one suitable for Pacific Northwest terrain, I told myself as the liquid in my stomach swirled around like a milkshake in a blender.

Beyond the rise of a short hill, the road became pea gravel for a much smoother, albeit noisier, ride. I glanced to my left at a man-made lake splotched with patches of algae. Two ducks splashed and quacked, giving each other a bath. The gravel road became an off-center horseshoe driveway in front of a sturdy, weather-worn barn in need of a paint job and a two-storey country house. I coasted to a stop in front of the house, where the porch swing and hummingbird feeder on the front deck made me ache for peaceful times.

I stepped out of the Saturn into brisk, mid-sixties air, grateful that the wind hadn't picked up yet to make it chilly. I tramped through soggy leaves in the yard as I walked around the side of the rustic home, past the apple tree that produced a good memory with Dee, teaching her how to can applesauce. Where the backyard sloped downhill toward the river, the branches of a gnarled elm rose up like a medicine man's arms waving around to summon ghosts. A tire swing hung from the thickest branch.

As I walked on past the wood shed to the left of the rear entrance, I stumbled. I regained my balance and looked down, frowning. The grass had been chewed up by the tires of a large truck that'd been backed up there recently. When I'd picked Dee up here late afternoon last Friday, the tread marks hadn't existed.

The wind chimes dangling around the back porch rattled in a breeze. Goose pimples sprouted on my arms and neck, but it wasn't from the abrupt chill in the air.

Something felt off.

I squatted in the flower garden next to the steps, where the custom-made clay gnome with a mischievous scowl flipped me the bird. Tipping the ornament back, I loosened the packed soil under its feet to dig up the hide-a-key container Dee had told me she'd buried there. All I unearthed were worms and potato bugs.

Something underneath the steps glinted in my peripheral vision. Shifting around, I looked at the sparkly object, then braced one hand on the stained deck to lean in closer. It was a

Bluetooth earpiece studded with diamonds. A few of the miniature stones were smeared with congealed blood.

I remembered the armed, suited men loitering outside Femme Ink across from Matt and me. One of them touched a similar accessory on his ear, while mumbling the syllables of a foreign language.

Rather than remove and contaminate the evidence indicative of a struggle, I took a picture of it with my iPhone instead. Then I walked back to my car, wiping moist dirt off my hands onto my jeans. I could use the set of lock picks I stored in the glove compartment with the gun safe to gain access.

I opened the passenger side door, then whirled around at a woman's voice.

"Can I help you?" the forty-something woman said in slightly accented English. She wore a low-cut beige cashmere sweater and a brown leather knee-length skirt that added some bulk to her waifish figure. The conservative clothing was both flattering and enough to make stock exchange analysts double-check their earnings to make sure they hadn't crashed. I wanted the tan, knee-high boots with the stiletto heels. Her hair was albino-white.

Who the hell are you, I almost snapped. "Good morning," I said instead, forcing my lips into a grin. It probably looked like bullshit, but it was all the courtesy I could manage to extend. I stopped reaching for the glove box, and popped the storage compartment between the seats open.

The woman descended the front steps on legs firmed to a perfection beyond the capabilities or schedule of an office executive. She'd danced professionally and probably worked out every day to keep her ass tight and muscles limber, I decided. Zumba, perhaps. Maybe pole dancing.

"This property is private," she told me, hugging an iPad in her arms.

Definitely German, maybe Dutch or Swedish. Although the polite authority in her tone wasn't defensive, her blue eyes glinted like icicles. I knew the soul of a cool, corporate lady when I saw one. For people like this, everything was business, including a human being's life.

I squirted a glob of sanitizer on my fingers and wiped my filthy hands off. "Hold on a sec," I said. "Checking out the back, I slipped on the leaves and fell." I tossed the small bottle to the floorboard and straightened. The corporate lady had stopped on the last step, otherwise I would've been taller than her by more than an inch.

"At breakfast in the diner back there," I continued, pointing over my shoulder in the direction of Carver, "the waitress told me this house might be for sale. It would make a perfect home for me and my life partner."

She gave me a respectful nod. "I'm sure it would. Unfortunately, it's sold."

"Oh, damn. Well, can I have one of your cards? Maybe there's another property similar to this one you can show me?"

"Sorry," she said, "I'm fresh out. But if you provide me with your phone number, I'll get in touch with you later in the week."

I rattled off a phone number that she tapped into her tablet computer with her long, square, flawlessly-manicured fingernails. They were painted with a glossy gold polish and reminded me of the vicious talons on a bird of prey. She also wore a ring on each finger.

"This is for an animal shelter," she noted. "Your place of employment, yes?"

"Uh-huh. That's the best place to reach me. I'm there forty-five, sometimes sixty hours a week. I manage it," I told her in a tone of voice that indicated no other vocation stacked up to caring for animals. "That's the other reason I want a house in the country," I added. "A place where my pets can, you know, roam free."

Closing the passenger door, I sidestepped around the hood of my car and turned to point an excited finger at the barn. I didn't turn my back to the woman entirely. "I could transform that into the perfect animal sanctuary." I beamed with pleasure. "Come on, let me show you."

I moved toward the barn, but her voice halted me before I could take two steps.

"No!" she said, the pitch of her voice threatening. "It's not permitted."

I froze, realizing that I'd missed her setting the iPad down, which left her hands free. The hand she'd tapped the pad with, her right hand, was poised on her hip, in easy reach of the small of her back. I'd assume a similar posture to throw a concealed knife.

"Okay," I said, shrugging disarmingly. "Maybe at the other property you show me, then."

I stepped over to the driver's door and opened it, but before I got in, I folded my arms casually on top of the car. "I didn't see the *For Sale* sign pulling in," I said. "What realty do you work for, Miss . . . ?"

"Apex," she told me, moving down off the last step, hands casually smoothing the sides of her skirt. "Jones."

"Thank you," I said, smirking at the unimaginative alias she'd pulled out of her ass, then I ducked into the Saturn.

"You're welcome," she said, bending over to give me one more look through the passenger window, her eyes narrowed.

I recognized her trained perception struggling to recall where she recognized me from. I gave the ignition a crank and revved the engine. Shifting into drive, I got the hell out of there before the bitch could place me in one of the pictures inside Dee's house.

I watched her in the rearview mirror as she hustled back to the steps to grab her iPad. The camera eye in the upper corner flashed. She'd taken a picture of my license plate to run later. Shit.

Reaching over, I got my Glock from the gun safe, and set it on my lap. I felt more secure.

Until I drove by the barn, and the woman's surge of anxiety I'd observed rattled my suspicions.

Once I turned onto the main road, I sped back toward Carver. I slowed down for an oncoming RV to pass, then turned into the general store lot. I pulled into a spot in a row reserved for long-term.

From the back seat, I grabbed my dark green Columbia Sportswear jacket. It was a size too big—perfect to conceal the shoulder rig I'd gotten from the glove box. I pulled that on, adjusted it for a comfortable fit, then slid the sidearm into the holster. I remembered a pair of latex gloves, my Leatherman, and some plastic baggies, too. The pocket tool was in a nylon sheath I clipped to my left hip. I stuffed the other items in my coat pockets.

The bell above the door jingled as I stepped inside the outpost. I turned left, stomped over to the aisle of coolers along the side wall, and opened a case to grab a bottle of water. A pair of overweight rednecks, one holding a Styrofoam container of bait, the other hefting a case of beer, wolf whistled at my ass.

"That'll be a dollar-five," the cashier said in a gravelly voice as he rang my purchase up on an antique register. No digital readout flashed. The total popped out from the top of the machine on small plastic tags.

I gave the old-timer a pair of twenties, which twisted the deep wrinkles of his face with confusion.

"That enough to rent a fishing boat for a few hours?" I said.

"Yes, ma'am. Can I interest you in some tackle as well?"

"Sure." I gave him another twenty.

His eyes brightened. A wide smile made his heavy jowls jiggle with delight. "Sales keep up like this, I'll be eating steak tonight."

FIVE

Matt Grudge

I SAT back down behind my desk and restarted the surveillance DVD on my laptop. The crisp digital footage from the camera above the ATM dragged on, slowly displaying a lineup of suspects between the occasional large vehicle that blocked the view. I hadn't watched this much TV since I was a kid. Bored out of my mind, the only thing that kept me watching, aside from searching for a murderer, was the assortment of characters from all walks of life that entered and exited Femme Ink.

A musician with an acoustic guitar slung over his back. Executives in serge suits. A little person wearing alligator boots. A pair of rockabilly models sashaying in flouncy fifties skirts. A girl in a tight v-neck sweater who looked as wholesome as a babysitter.

About two hours later the girl-next-door type walked out, her lips stretched in a wide smile. She looked too young to get inked legally. I supposed she could've conned or seduced an artist into letting her get a tat. Then a relative could have paid the shop a visit, and a disagreement over liability and money turned violent and deadly.

I recognized a mixed martial arts fighter I'd seen featured in an edition of the *Portland Mercury*. He toted a toddler in his arms. The kid swiveled his head around, taking in all of the bustling street activity. A nun on her way out paused to play with him. A nun in a tattoo parlor? I thought nuns didn't get tattooed because it mutilated "the temple of God" that was their body.

I fingered the mouse and moved the pointer to track back. When the best position of the nun's face appeared, I clicked a screen capture, then enlarged that with a freeware imaging program. Eyes narrowed, I glared suspiciously at the religious woman. Then I returned to the footage.

An attractive young woman with her hair up, a loose strand of it in her mouth, read a book as she shuffled toward the entrance from the cafe. She bumped into the sister. After apologizing and getting a nod with a smile from the sister, the bookworm continued on her way.

Then the door to the parlor swung open, swiftly enough that the MMA fighter wrapped both arms around the kid and shifted sideways to avoid it. The nun turned her head to watch.

A bald tattoo artist I recognized from the photographs in the shop came crashing through the entrance, pulling a rodent-faced guy with greasy long hair out by his ear. Jerking and squirming, the guy tried to resist, even threw a blind punch around. The artist casually tilted his face to dodge the wild blow. Grabbing the guy's arm, the artist contorted it up at an agonizing angle. The unwanted customer winced, his lips flapping with curses and screams of pain.

I paused the image and took a screen capture. This was too big of a break in the case to wait for tonight.

I called Leslie's cell. Her voicemail answered. "Shit," I said, flipping my phone shut and tossing it on my desk. Cropping the faces of the artist and patron into separate jpeg files, I attached them with a text to Leslie.

I played the rest of the incident. The artist released the patron, who walked away up the street, massaging his grappled shoulder. The nun and MMA guy continued to observe the scene. Hard to tell if they were fascinated by the artist or the asshole he'd kicked out. The nun tousled the kid's hair before the fighter waved so long and ducked inside the parlor.

I closed the laptop screen and stood up to pace around, glaring at my cell phone. "Come on, Leslie. Call back, dammit."

I tried the landline at the loft. Voicemail answered there, also.

I stuffed my cell phone in the side pocket of my jeans, pulled my jacket on, and strode into the outer office, pausing to glance at the picture behind Leslie's desk. It concealed our weapons safe. I decided to forego packing a sidearm, a blade, or a taser and locked up to leave.

A short drive up to the Pearl District took me into the trendy neighborhood where Leslie had her loft, and the gym she favored to blow off steam. The facility took up the top floor of a modern condo tower. When I stepped through the double glass doors, the air conditioner propelled the odors of deodorant and sweat up my nostrils. Paramore's "Misery Business" thumped from the Bose speakers mounted around the establishment.

At the service desk to the left that featured a glass case full of tank tops and overpriced water bottles, I said hi to the counter girl with the stacks of assorted bracelets on her wrists. "Have you seen Leslie?" I asked.

She looked up from one of the motorcycle magazines she always perused. "Nope."

"It's busy in here today," I said. "Can you check the locker room in case she slipped past you? I'll watch the register."

She dropped the magazine on the counter, then kicked off the high-legged chair. "Please would be nice," she muttered.

"Pretty-fucking-please with sugar," I said with a forced grin.

"Okay, okay. Don't be a dick." She went to the ladies' room.

I waited amidst the clank of free weights and the whir from the rows of treadmills, bicycle machines, stair climbers, and rowing machines in motion. A Pilates class in session made me think of Pepper's sexual flexibility. Two boxers in padded gear exchanged blows in the ring while their trainers barked out strategies.

I studied the fit people strengthening and toning their bodies. Most of them wore earbuds, listening to their own playlists, or flipped through magazine pages, or tapped electronic readers as they worked out. What really attracted my attention was the abundance of tattoos: back pieces of a family crest, the Grim Reaper shouldering his scythe, and a magician juggling fire; the bust of a lady vampire on the biceps of a Goth in the Pilates class; military service medals on the massive, ropy arms of a weightlifter; chest pieces of birds, mazes, and comic book characters; sleeves composed of exotic flowers, pinups, or precious stones. My favorite was a black and gray portrait of Humphrey Bogart and Ingrid Bergman from *Casablanca* on the ripped lower torso of a woman in a pink sports bra and red boxer shorts doing pull-ups.

Maybe two people out of the thirty-plus group didn't have any ink. Then again, maybe their exercise clothes covered it up, or the tat branded a body part inappropriate to bare in public.

I felt a soft whack on the back of my head and spun around. The punk counter girl had returned. "She's not here," she told me, lowering her rolled-up mag that she'd smacked me with.

"You sure? Long, raven-black hair. American Indian. Feather and barbed wire tattoo on her upper left bicep."

"And a phoenix with fiery wings outstretched on her abs," she finished.

"Yeah."

"Are you deaf, detective boy? She's. Not. Here."

"Alright. Thanks. Look," I said, taking out my cell phone and bringing up the profile of the artist from Femme Ink on the display. "I was admiring the ink around here and it got me wondering if you refer any customers to local tattoo shops. Maybe you recognize this artist?" I showed her the image.

She tapped her chin with her index finger. Her fingernails were chewed down to the quick. Her big hazel eyes blinked in a sign of recognition. "Do you know that vegan deli on Division?" she asked. "Papa G's."

"Sure."

"A month or so ago, I was eating dinner there with a girlfriend. He was the drummer in a band playing that night."

I closed the phone and tucked it in my pocket. "Thank you."

"Piece of advice," the counter girl offered as I turned to leave. "You shouldn't ogle some of the people, or their tats, in here. See that ox kickboxing the heavy bag? He's been scoping you out ever since you came in."

"I'm sure he is. He made the mistake of caressing Leslie's cheek during a sparring session," I said, then chuckled. "Dirtbag probably wants a rematch to see how fast she can knock him the hell out again."

SIX

Leslie Crow

I APPROACHED the mouth of the stream that dumped into the Clackamas River from the lake on Dee's property. A hundred yards away, I turned the motor off and propelled the boat with an oar; it glided across the calm water until, satisfied, I anchored the boat, baited a hook, cast the line, and wedged the pole in the slats.

I stood up and placed a foot on the port side. Arms spread, I waited for the listing motion my weight shift caused to subside. I leapt up onto the bank, landing in a crouch inside the field of high grass, my boots squishing into the marshy ground. Staying low, I jogged along the stream. I heard frogs croaking and spotted a swampy area ahead, slimy with algae and spiked with reeds. I jumped across and stopped.

I could see the fenced-in area behind the barn. I pulled the Glock out, barrel angled down as I moved in closer. To my left Dee's gold and white Palomino, Hammer, quenched his thirst with sloppy, wet gulps from a water trough. The parade horse stopped drinking, whinnied, tossed his head, then galloped into the stables.

My eyes panned around for sentries. I sniffed the air to detect careless giveaways, like cigarette smoke. I got a whiff of the fresh manure apples Hammer had dropped near the horse walker.

Holstering the pistol, I flung my leg up onto the fence to climb over, then quickly redrew the firearm as my feet touched down on the other side. I crept toward the wide stable entrance, the Glock aimed high in a two-handed grip. A footstep inside, I paused a few seconds while my sight adjusted to the dusky interior.

The earthy smell of grain, damp hay, and manure filled my nostrils. I moved my back up against the concrete wall on my right, in case Hammer decided to come charging through.

Three-quarters along the wide concrete walkway, I slipped. Reaching out for the side rail with my right hand, I kept the gun clenched in my left. The floor was drenched with water. I shuffled to regain my footing, then pushed on.

The farther I walked into the passageway, the more pungent the odor of an industrial-strength sanitizer grew. I breathed through my mouth to prevent gagging, but still I felt the lining of my throat become as abrasive as sandpaper, and the blood vessels in my head throbbed and pulsated.

The passageway ended at a T-junction. I looked straight up at a massive web suspended between support beams and square columns. A spider as big as my fist clung to the silk strands, spinning a cocoon around paralyzed prey. I anticipated that a similar fate awaited me unless I conducted this search quickly.

A strong wind howled through the drafty corridor. I heard the soft creaking as the barn settled. The chemical smell dissipated. Sweat beaded my forehead.

I raised the Glock back up in both hands to cover my twelve o'clock, and continued scanning for clues.

Turning left, I stepped slowly past three stalls. The gate to the first box was closed. Saddles and tools for shoeing horses hung from the walls. I spotted a high shelf lined with framed pictures of Dee-Dee and Hammer attending the Oregon State Fair and the St. Paul Rodeo. Polished plaques and frilly ribbons were mounted above those to complete Dee-Dee's shrine for her horse. Not allowing sentiment to blur my objective, I moved on.

A cinder block propped the door to the second stall open. The floor was covered with straw. A feed trough on the right side of the box needed refilling. I tracked my eyes back to the straw because I discerned something out of the ordinary. It could've been the imprint of a human body with its limbs spread. I moved in for a closer look, searching for bloodstains on the straw, but didn't see any.

Turning around, I peered left, then right along the passage before I walked back out.

Hammer stood in the last box, and eyed me warily as I sidestepped by.

Fifteen feet farther, I paused at a closed gate that gave access to the main floor of the barn. Keeping the wide open target area and massive double doors beyond covered with the Glock in my right hand, I reached for the latch with my left.

When I pushed the latch in, my fingers mashed a putty-like substance in the wood.

I holstered the sidearm and got my Leatherman out. Using the clip-point blade, I picked at the hole someone had filled with putty. Once I'd scraped most of the rubbery compound out, I felt the gap with my finger. The way in which the wood was splintered around the hole told me it had been made by small arms fire. I looked along the gate and noticed it was peppered with filled-in bullet holes.

I slipped the tool back in its pouch and pushed the gate open. Drawing my pistol, I moved out onto the main floor, then kicked the gate shut behind me. The wood plank flooring had been hosed down. Gusts of the rising wind shifted a row of chains hung from the meat hooks in the ceiling rafters. The clinking sound gave me chills. The barn used to be a slaughterhouse before Dee-Dee had it refitted to be a stable.

I headed for the staircase to my far right. Climbing the creaky steps, I ascended into the loft.

The machete lying on the floor was out of place. Dee was downright anal about tools, especially sharp ones, being stored properly. I looked at a pulley system that could be positioned either above the main floor or the stalls, and panned narrowed eyes around stacks of straw bales. Another abnormal item caught my attention.

I holstered the Glock and unsheathed my Leatherman. I also snatched a plastic Baggie from my jacket pocket. I thumbed the Leatherman's small flathead screwdriver out and used it to carefully pick up the spent brass from a high-caliber round, its bronze color almost camouflaged by the golden straw. I dropped the bullet casing in the Baggie, sealed it, then scribbled the date, time, location, and my signature on it with a permanent marker. Stuffing the evidence in my jeans pocket, I looked harder at the floor around the stacked bales. I recognized knee prints in the dirt and dust.

A shooter had used the loft for a sniper's nest. Who were they shooting at in Dee's barn?

One of the double doors swung open.

"Fuck," I mouthed. Ducking down out of sight, I peered around the corner.

A big guy in grimy overalls stood with his back to me, shouting in Russian at someone outside. I recognized the voice of the corporate lady shouting back at him, also in Russian. Then I heard tires spitting gravel and a rumbling engine grow distant.

Where was she going?

The red-headed giant slammed the door shut and turned around. He carried a toolbox in his right hand.

He stomped toward the stairs with the lumbering gait of a weightlifter. His muscles bulged under the flannel shirt he wore underneath the overalls. A little more than ten feet away from the stairs, he stopped and looked up at the loft. The expression on his beaten, weathered face resembled that of a guard dog scenting fear.

As I went to pocket the marker, it slipped from my sweaty fingers. In heart-wrenching slow motion the Sharpie fell through the planks, tumbled in the air, then landed with a soft tap.

I heard the clomp of his feet bounding up the stairs. Desperately I looked around, then seized the free end of the pulley rope, tied a loop, and threw it at the landing just at the top of the steps.

The ape bellowed a command. In the corner of my eye I saw the pistol he leveled at me. I sucked in a quick breath as a spurt of flame flashed from the barrel.

I dropped to one knee. The bullet whistled overhead. Launching my shoulder into a tackle, I shoved the bales nearest me over the side of the loft.

The snare tightened around the goliath's ankle. The rope snaked through the pulley and the weight of the falling bales hoisted him upside down. Arms flailing, he dropped the gun and it fell into the second stall. His head wobbled at a height even with a speed bag. He tried to reach out and grab me, but I stayed beyond his reach. The Russian spewing from his mouth peppered with spittle sounded really nasty.

I picked the machete up off the floor and he shut up. "Speak English?" I asked.

The behemoth began to shake his head. I let him wag "no" once, then threw a right hook into his mouth. My human skull ring cut his lip open and blood dribbled down into his nostril.

"Bitch," he said, blowing blood out of his nose.

I followed up with a backhand that left a red welt across his cheek. "You better know more than profanity. Who the hell are you people? What's going on here?"

"I *know* you from photograph in house," he told me, giving me a shark's grin.

I drove a punch into his pearly whites. It chipped one of his upper teeth. The fragment went flying.

"Go ahead," he said, chuckling like a comedian schmoozing a comedy club audience. "Use me for punching bag all day. I won't speak. And you can't kill me. You American cops play by too many rules."

The pulley was attached to an arm I unlocked. I gave the Russian a shove from behind. He cursed some more as the makeshift block and tackle swiveled to suspend his body twenty feet above the ground.

"You're not up on your hard-boiled ethics," I called out. "Private eyes like me make our own rules."

"Fall won't kill me," he said with a whimper.

"You're right," I said, then cut the rope with the machete.

His screaming broke off abruptly when his body smashed into the hardwood floor head first with a painful cracking sound, like a stalk of celery snapped in half.

"Landing wrong might break your neck, though."

I wiped my prints off the machete handle and set it down approximately where it'd originally been. Trotting down the stairs, I alternated aiming the Glock from the Russian to the double doors, in case he wasn't alone.

Once I reached his body, I moved in a wide circle around him. His chest was still moving. I knelt down beside his unconscious form. Tucking the end of the gun barrel underneath his chin, I patted his pockets down.

No wallet.

His shoulder ball and socket joint protruded through the skin at an agonizing angle. That was the break I'd heard. In a way I was glad. If the fall had killed him, I would've had to call the cops to report it.

With the lackey incapacitated, I continued the search for leads.

I returned to the T-junction on the other end of the stables, then proceeded down the corridor where the chemical solvent odor was strongest. My sense of smell had adjusted to the stench by now. The man-sized hallway ended at a steel door Dee-Dee kept locked because it led to her machine shop. The deadbolt was turned to act as a doorstop.

Wind slammed the latch against the thick metallic frame. The beat added an additional layer of fear to my erratic heartbeat. I shuffled toward the door. Beads of sweat slid down my forehead.

I kicked the door in and burst through the archway. The floor had been doused and sanitized. The saw blades and tools attached to the wall behind a workbench gleamed. They also reeked from being cleaned recently with a bleach-based solution.

I stepped over to the foyer that connected the side entrance to another door. Twisting the ornate block of wood, I unlatched the pantry door. The interior was pitch black. I reached up and tugged a string to turn on the naked bulb in the low ceiling socket. The soft, 60-watt glow illuminated rows of shelves stocked with canned goods and jars of fruit and veggies.

Moving toward the large chest freezer that occupied the entire width of the far wall, I hefted the lid open. Cold air blasted upward. I fanned the vapors aside with the Glock. Bags of corn, peas, chicken breasts, a huge turkey, and quarts of ice cream insulted my fear.

Did you really expect to find dissected body parts or a corpse in the ice chest?

I walked outside. Inhaling several deep breaths of the crisp, fresh air purged my lungs. I headed for the rusted barrel and compost pile near the right side of the main house. The ripe smell of discarded produce breaking down into a moldy sludge was a comforting aroma compared to the barn's atmosphere.

Kneeling down in the spongy grass and soil, I picked up some materials someone had probably intended to burn. Only the rainstorm last night had prevented that. Holstering the Glock, I snapped on the latex gloves, then rummaged.

I fingered shreds of clothing. Sorting through the articles, I found and read the labels: Armani, Ralph Lauren . . . The care instructions and sizes were printed in a foreign alphabet.

On the bottom of the pile I uncovered half of a suit jacket that was fairly dry. Straightening, I snapped the material loose, then reached into the inside pocket. I withdrew a greeting card-sized envelope and a rolled up newspaper. I stowed the items beneath my coat, tucked into my jeans at the small of my back.

An engine purr whipped me around. A silver BMW came rolling over the hill on the driveway. I bolted for the long grass, then sprinted to the river.

I skidded to a halt on the bank. Jumping into the boat would capsize it. I waded into the freezing water. The current lapped up to my thighs. Clamping my lips shut to keep a groan of discomfort lodged in my throat, I clambered over the gunwale, reeled in the fishing line, and pulled up the small anchor.

I gave the outboard motor a tug. It didn't start. I gave it a harder pull, adding a little elbow grease. The engine still wouldn't turn over.

The grass and reeds on the bank rustled. I twisted around, sidearm drawn. A squirrel twitched its tail at me, then darted back into the brush.

"Come on, you *son of a—*" I said, teeth chattering. I gave the cord another yank. Water bubbled out from the stern as the propeller finally began to spin. Maneuvering out to the center of the river, I sped away as fast as the compact engine could go. Every ten feet I threw a glance over my shoulder to make sure no one appeared on the embankment to spot my getaway.

SEVEN

Matt Grudge

I SQUEEZED my plain sedan into a compact spot on the south side of Southeast Twelfth and Stark. Traffic was thick and carcinogenic with the post-lunch crowd rushing back to work. I checked my cell for any messages or texts; Pepper had left a message about an hour ago. The time was 1:03 p.m.

I waited for the light behind me for east and westbound traffic to turn red before I got out of my car. Stepping up onto the sidewalk, I sauntered between a row of elm trees and a closed elementary school, feeling a twinge of remorse for the gutted structure as I waited for the pedestrian light to click to *Walk*. I trotted across the busy side street, but not fast enough for a motorist making a right turn. He leaned on his horn. Although the windows were up, I heard the string of curses the driver flung at my dashing back.

A skater on his board raced alongside me. "That dude's got issues," he said.

Leaping up onto the curb across the street, I drilled a nasty look into the vehicle as it sped past. I wanted to yell back at the driver, but working a case demanded that I maintain a low profile.

I walked past storefronts in a poured concrete mini-mall that catered to Portland's vegan community: The Sweetpea Baking Company, Herbivore Clothing, Food Fight! Grocery, and my destination, Scapegoat Tattoo. Pulling the tattoo shop door open, I held it for a pair of twenty-something girls barging out, one a brunette, the other a blonde with blue streaks. Holding hands, they bopped up the street. Their forearms were bandaged.

The tangy fragrance of citrus teased my nostrils as I approached the counter—a restored walnut desk sitting kitty-corner on the left. The redhead tucked away behind it with a pencil stuck in her fiery bob and a pierced septum flashed me a sunny smile. She was gently rubbing a glob of aftercare cream over samurai wielding swords, koi fish, and dancing geisha that swirled around a full-color sleeve on her left arm. The top buttons of the low-cut, bleached denim vest she wore were undone to show off her cleavage. "Can I help you?" she asked.

I peered over her head at the four artists in booths behind her, tattoo machines buzzing away. I grinned as I spotted the tattooist I'd been searching for. "I need to speak with that artist, please," I said, nodding toward him.

"The piece he's doing might take another hour," the receptionist told me. "After that, though, he doesn't have another appointment until four."

"I'm happy to wait." I pulled out a business card embossed with Alternative Investigations, my name, Leslie's name, our phone numbers, and our skull and filigree logo. Snatching a pen from the counter, I inscribed *Dee-Dee Magnolia?* on the back. "Give this to him," I said, offering her the card and a pair of ten dollar bills.

Her green-mascaraed eyes widened at the tip, her long, silver-painted nails fingering the card. She stuffed the cash in the side pocket of her brown leather hip-huggers, the motion tugging their waistline low enough for me to see groupings of black stars with golden sparkles shooting up from the top of her pubis. "Sure thing, sweetie."

Hopping down off her stool, the redhead hipped over to the bald inker's area. I browsed the body jewelry in the swivel display case on the counter, pretending not to notice her round, sensual curves and hollows. They roused a memory of earlier pleasure and I felt guilty regret for mistreating Pepper's sexuality.

I slouched down on a black and green pleather sectional next to the antique desk. I felt sweat in my armpits gelling my deodorant into a slimy ooze and I could tell my face was flushed. The heat was up too high. Okay, the thermostat wasn't the only element affecting my body chemistry.

Mounted on the wall across from me in a cherry wood frame was a huge picture of Dee-Dee posed semi-nude for PETA's "I'd Rather Go Naked Than Wear Fur" campaign. The portrait gave me the opportunity to read the other set of letters tattooed on her left knuckles: B-O-M-B.

Fire bomb, huh. Yeah, I thought, *that's what her death dropped on my partnership with Leslie.*

I grabbed an issue of *Inked* from the small table by the sectional. Diablo Cody's frank sensuality seared the cover. I perused the magazine, then tossed it back on the table. The rhythmic hum of the tattoo machines, paired with the over-warm temperature, was starting to put me into a daze.

An attractive curly-haired brunette entered the parlor. She wore a tie-dyed blouse and denim bell bottoms with sandals under lime green socks dotted with smiling pig faces. She grilled the redhead about whether or not she'd come to the right place to get a cruelty-free tattoo.

"Of course," the redhead said. "Just a sec." She hustled to the nearest station and grabbed two plastic bottles. Offering one to the customer, she rotated the ingredients label around. "This pigment is made from plant derivatives, not from animal bones burned down to charcoal."

"What about the carrier solution?" the older woman asked.

"The glycerin is from vegetable sources," the receptionist replied, "not animal fats."

The lady withdrew a folded sheet of graph paper from her back pocket. Unfolding it, she set the paper down on the countertop and smoothed the wrinkles out. "I'd like this to be free drawn on my left biceps."

"Absolutely . . . Is this a heartbeat?"

"My *first* granddaughter's fetal heartbeat," the brunette said.

Streaks of rain were slashing the windows when the bald tattoo artist finally stepped around the counter. "Where do you want to talk?" he asked me. He had on an ink-stained white cotton sweater and black jeans. A pair of red dice with white dots tattooed on his neck rolled into motion over his jugular when he spoke. I wondered what the tat represented—chance, random values, or shooting the odds?

Pieces of my profession, I thought.

"Can I buy you a late lunch, or a cup of coffee?" I asked as I stood.

"Nope," the tattoo artist said. "Got that covered, thanks. And coffee makes my hands shake. I just want to get this over with."

"There an office in back?" I asked.

"Follow me."

At the end of a compact hallway behind the tattooing booths, we took a sharp right into a room cramped with an IKEA desk, two chairs, and stacks of supply boxes. I took a seat in the plastic chair by the door, while the artist took the plush swivel chair at the cluttered desk. Reaching across the desk to lift a small cooler onto on the blotter, he opened the lid and took out a large Rubbermaid bottle filled with pink, frothy liquid and chunks of fruit. After shaking it up, he opened the top, took a long gulp, then sighed.

"Name's Reggie," he said as he read my business card. "I want to make this clear, Grudge. If something you uncover about Dee's murder sees print and disgraces her rep, I will throw you a beating."

"That won't be a problem, Reggie," I told him. "I know how much it sucks when local newspapers drag a reputation through the mud or twist events for good copy or sensationalism. I'm a detective trying to find a killer, not a glory hound posing for publicity."

"I've heard you don't care for the nickname Stumptown's given you. Fair enough," Reggie said before throwing back more of his protein shake. "Now, what can I do for you?"

I leaned forward in the plastic patio chair, elbows braced on my knees. "I'm looking into the events around Dee-Dee's murder for my partner," I said. "They were close. And since the police have put an airtight seal on the crime scene, even squelching the media from reporting the murder, I'm looking at anything obscure or suspicious for a lead."

"Leslie and Dee were like sisters."

"Yes," I said.

Reggie stroked his salt-and-pepper goatee, then leaned back, resting his hiking boots on the top of a medium-sized crate. "Maybe there are details too explicit for public consumption," he said, "or being withheld to avoid mass panic?"

"You're right. Another thing they're probably trying to prevent is cranks calling in for attention. Those precautions aside, though," I said, "it doesn't explain a cover-up."

"You're not one of those paranoid conspiracy nuts, are you, Grudge?"

"I want the perpetrators apprehended before Leslie gets them alone. As emotionally unstable as she is right now, not to mention wild, revenge won't have a limit, and she could go on a killing spree. What will that do for the tattoo culture, huh?"

Reggie held his hands up in a gesture of surrender. "Say no more. I just don't know what I can tell you. I left early that afternoon to meet my kid's teacher at a conference."

"On the day of the murder between one and two p.m., you tossed a patron out of Femme Ink," I said. "What can you tell me about him? Why did you eject the scumbag?"

"Skinhead claiming that he'd found religion," Reggie said. "Wanted a tattoo he'd earned in prison covered up with new ink."

"I'm betting this didn't sit well with Dee-Dee."

"Hell, no. Once a Nazi, always a Nazi. She asked me to kick the bastard out."

"Do you think he could've came back to the shop later and killed her?" I asked.

He shrugged. "Anything's possible. I don't think so, though. I got the impression his incarceration dulled his teeth. All bark and no bite."

"What if I wanted to find this lowlife to question him? Would there be a record opened at Femme Ink with his address, maybe even a credit card number for a deposit?"

"You'd have to ask Pepper," Reggie told me. "She handles all the paperwork."

I sighed. "Okay. I'll have to get in touch with her."

"The two of you go way back, huh. Friends with benefits," Reggie said, giving me a smile that indicated he could tell when karma was a bitch.

"Yeah, so?" I snapped. "I don't see how that's any of your goddamn business."

"Be careful if you question Pepper like she's a hostile suspect," Reggie told me. "She isn't the same girl, ever since returning from Europe."

"What's that supposed to mean?"

"Pepper confronted a patron outside one of the bars where I moonlight as a bouncer. Not that the prick didn't deserve it. He tried to follow Pepper to her car, claiming that she was drunk, which she wasn't. I discovered a blade in his coat. Pepper said he pulled it on her, but that doesn't warrant what she did to defend herself."

"Which was . . . ?"

"She drove a rapid series of rabbit punches into the base of his skull, broke his jaw. The last time I saw a woman of that weight class put an opponent down so fast was Gina Carano in her MMA debut bout."

Good for Pepper, I thought. Still, a sympathetic twinge rippled across my aching ribs, reminding me of the force behind Pepper's kick when she threw me out of the parlor. I stood to leave. "Thank you, Reggie. Keep my card. If you think of anything else that might help, give me a call."

"I'll give you some advice now."

I pulled my coat on and nodded for him to go ahead.

"Next time you drop by, don't wear genuine leather in here. It's appalling to my customers. As for you investigating Dee's murder . . . I'm not a . . . private dick, but with no access to the evidence to lead to any suspects, you're reaching for motives in a vacuum. You're headed down a blind alley with a bull's-eye on your back."

"Sorry about the dead animal skin," I said, zipping up my jacket. "I'll make a note. And you're right about the aspects of this case . . ." I gave the hard-core vegan a smug glare. "But when a PI is driven, discouraged, or warned to watch his step, it only makes him keep going." I walked away.

•

I PULLED into the loading zone behind Femme Ink. Remembering Pepper's text from earlier, I checked it for any tip-offs to her mood. My chances of convincing her to let me see the skinhead's application were probably zero, but I had to try.

Panic tightened my grip on my cell phone as I read: *They've broken in. Tossing the studio. Looking for me. Get your ass over here!*

Muscles tensing, I looked to the rear entrance. It'd been jimmied. The door banged open and shut in gusts of wind howling through the alley. My skin tingled as an adrenaline rush surged through my veins. I yanked the emergency brake up and switched the engine off and opened the door to climb out, only the seatbelt I'd forgotten to unlatch stopped me. Cursing in a whisper, I unclasped the strap and yanked it off. I piled out of the car, not bothering to double-tap the button on the key fob. The beep of the alarm system engaging might've warned the intruders inside.

I jogged up the wheelchair ramp, then pressed my back against the sooty bricks beside the door, feeling the pounding of my heartbeat as I wiped sweaty palms on the thighs of my ratty jeans. Seizing a deep breath, I pivoted around the doorframe and ducked as I stepped just inside the parlor, in case a shooter waited in the shadows. I listened for rustles indicating movement, or thuds suggesting furniture being bumped and smashed. Inhaling, I caught a disinfectant odor.

The yellow, honeycomb-patterned vinyl floor between the main studio ahead and the stairs to my left that led up to the storage room and studio apartment was littered with boxes that'd been thrown, trampled, or dented. A skateboard deck featuring one of Dee-Dee's Celtic designs that normally hung on a wall in the waiting area lay flat, its surface scuffed like it'd just been ridden in a competition.

Slowly I straightened, then skirted the wreckage as quietly as possible. The worn-out soles of my sneakers barely made a sound—until I reached the pile of shattered glass. A few shards crunched when I stepped on them with the toe of my shoe.

The huge frames that'd featured collages of memories from the parlor had been destroyed. Pictures were scattered, bent, or torn up all over the carpet. Dropping to one knee, I picked through some of the photos. I found a couple of Leslie and Dee-Dee, and the one of Pepper inking my first tat, and pocketed them for safekeeping. So I'd tampered with a crime scene to preserve a few sentimental mementos. The DA or the cops could charge me, but I thought a little pilferage was low on their radar right now.

My head jerked toward a plopping sound. It came from the left, near the tattoo station covered in fingerprint powder. I rose carefully to move over there. The blinds were closed, concealing me from the everyday traffic outside.

Glass shards from the front counter formed a kaleidoscope of ruin. The framed flash on the partition behind it had been taken down, the tattoo photos removed so the frames could be searched. All of the mechanical pencils and pens in a ceramic holder were scattered about, dismantled.

Spotting a puddle of black ink on the carpet just in time, I sidestepped the mess, waving my arms out like I was walking a tightrope. That would've been good, leaving my shoe impression in the crime scene.

I breathed shallowly. I didn't want to irritate my allergy to fingerprint powder and throw my lungs up in another coughing fit. I heaved a sigh of relief when I realized the excess powder had been cleaned up. Unfortunately, the tattoo station had been torn apart. All of the drawers had been pulled out, the contents of each one dumped everywhere. Even the lightbulb for the desktop lamp had been removed and crushed.

The sound I'd heard ended up being a Starbucks coffee cup that appeared to have fallen off the edge of the desk. The lid had popped off, the creamy tan remnants pooling near a row of filing cabinets tucked away to the left of the station. I hopped over the puddle of coffee, landing in front of the drawers and catching myself with a hand on the cabinet. The hollow vibration I felt through my palm disappointed me before I even pulled the cabinets out.

All of the files were gone.

I flinched as my cell phone chirped with a text message tone. I'd forgotten to switch it to mute. Whirling, I braced my back up against the filing cabinet, feeling the cold metal pressing against my spine. The tattoo studio replied to my paranoid reflexes with the silence of a morgue—where I'd end up if I kept making reckless mistakes.

I took a deep breath and read the display. A new message from Pepper said: *R U HERE YET! I'm in the bathroom upstairs.*

I thumbed a reply: *I'm coming up.*

Before pressing Send, I stopped cold. Anyone could be using Pepper's handset to send me messages and lead me into a trap.

I retraced my steps back to the foot of the stairs. The third step up whined a creak that echoed up through the stairwell. My nerves tingled.

I reached the landing for the second floor, and stared through the open door to the storage area. Sweat slid down my temple, tickling my peripheral vision. I found myself in the ideal position for an ambush. If a shooter stashed away behind the boxes in the storeroom disabled me with the first shot, accomplices could open fire from the top and bottom of the stairs, cutting me to shreds.

Teeth clenched, I bolted up the next flight of stairs. I shouldered the unlatched door open, dropped into a squat, then forward rolled into the compact kitchen. Something slimy squished under my knee.

The antique refrigerator door stood open. Cockroaches scattered all over the discarded vegetables on the linoleum floor.

The cupboards and drawers had been searched also. The dishes and glasses were intact, while the silverware and junk drawers were dumped out on the countertop and dining nook table.

I crept into the bedroom. The edges of the carpet all along the baseboards had been cut and pulled out from the wall. The bamboo shelf hung from one nail, its collection of shot glasses shattered on the dresser. I gulped.

The bed had been slashed to ribbons. Tufts of stuffing lay everywhere. The lightbulbs in the lamp on the nightstand and in the overhead fan had been taken out and broken. The nightstand had been pulled out from the wall and the faceplate on the power outlet behind it had been removed.

What were the intruders looking for? With all the smashed frames downstairs I'd thought it was a document of some kind, but with the writing utensils, lightbulbs, and now the exposed electrical outlets, I began to wonder if someone was searching for surveillance gear, a bug. And intruders wouldn't tear a place apart for that.

I heard a hushed whimper from the bathroom, and my gut knotted. On my way there, I spotted Pepper's eyeglasses on the floor beyond the ravaged bed; one of the earpieces was snapped clean off, the lenses cracked.

I grasped the knob and gave it a turn. Locked. Standing back, I put all of my 220 pounds of muscle behind a kick near the latch. The jamb groaned and splintered, but the solid wood held. Two more kicks and an elbow ram flung it open.

Her entire body shaking, Pepper sat huddled in the corner by the claw-footed bathtub, in nothing but hot pink cotton panties and a blouse that was torn apart at the shoulders. Blood seeped from her nostril and a scrape down her cheek. Sopping wet hair dripped water down her cheeks that mingled with tears of fright. The desperation in her nearsighted stare indicated she'd survived a terrifying ordeal.

She didn't intend to go through that hell again without a fight. Swinging the bat choked in her fists in wild arcs, she yelled, "Come and get it, fuckers." Her swollen lower lip quivered. "Want a piece of me, you'll bleed for it first."

"Pepper, it's Matt. I got your messages. Drop the bat."

"What messages? Wasn't I clear enough this morning? Get out. It's because of you they did this. All they kept repeating was, 'Where did he plant the bug?' or 'What did he want to know about the Magnolia murder?' This is all your fault, Matt," she shouted.

"If you didn't text me," I said, "then they sure as shit did. We need to get out of here now."

"I've been sitting too long," she told me. "My legs are too numb."

"Stop pretending to hit a homer and I'll carry you."

She tossed the bat aside. It bounced on the linoleum. I stepped forward, kicking the improvised weapon out of my path, and knelt to cinch my hands around Pepper's hips and pull her up over my shoulder in a fireman's carry.

In the foyer something halted my tracks and I took a step back to compensate. I heard wood scrape on wood or a fixture, and my muscles tensed. Snapping a look over my empty shoulder, I saw Pepper in my peripheral vision, reaching onto a coat rack.

"What the hell are you doing?" I said. "We need to keep moving."

"Bastards smashed my glasses. My contact lenses are in my purse. Okay, I got it. Go."

I blew a strand of her loose hair that'd gotten caught in my whiskers out with my nose, then turned back around to head for the stairs.

"That better not've been a grunt of exertion," Pepper said.

"You weigh nothing."

"Compliments won't get you laid," she said, then smacked me on the ass. "Move."

I'd reached the landing without banging Pepper's head on a fixture, but I was beginning to have second thoughts. Maybe just a little thump would encourage her to express some gratitude. Considering I'd performed cunnilingus on her earlier. I kept my mouth shut. I didn't need to piss away a chance to redeem a relationship I'd taken for granted.

Clearing the rear entrance, I hustled down the ramp, Pepper's tits bouncing on my back. She wasn't wearing a bra. I dug my keyring from my pocket and unlocked my car. I eased her into the passenger seat. "Watch your fingers," I said, slamming the door closed.

I raced around the back of the sedan, jumped in behind the wheel. Revving the engine, I spot-checked the rearview mirror. The entrance to the alley was clear. I peeled out backward onto Grand.

Fleeing the scene, I maneuvered for I-84 East. I brought the car to a hard, jarring stop behind one of the two lines of other vehicles waiting for a green light to enter the merge ramp. We were a good nine cars back from the signal. The rider on a chopper in front of us kept revving his engine. It sounded like an out-of-tune brass orchestra.

Pepper's head frantically swiveled, flashing tense glances behind us and to both sides of the car. I heard one of the bones in her neck crackle and pop. "You've got to be shitting me," she grumbled. "This is a horrible getaway route. You're crazy."

A driver up ahead leaned on their horn at the motorist in front of them who, not paying attention, had missed their turn to go. I could smell the exhaust fumes drifting in through the power windows I'd cracked open to help cool off. Either the risk involved back at the parlor or the peach scent of Pepper's shampoo was making my internal temperature rise like a heat wave in July, even in this overcast, drizzly, late afternoon in late September.

Her rapid breathing was approaching hyperventilation. "Try to relax," I said reassuringly. "I'll get you to a safe place. You better put your contacts in before we get on the freeway."

"If we need to stop or slow down," Pepper said, her tone argumentative, "it'll make it all too easy for the bastards to cap your ass and snatch me."

Gripping the rearview mirror, Pepper turned it toward her and scrutinized her irises for any dirt or particulates. Widening her eyes one at a time, she gently positioned the contacts on her eyeballs. Then she twisted the mirror back.

Enough raindrops had coated the windshield to distort the glow of the traffic light. I twisted the wipers on to low. The fuel gauge light lit up.

"Not in front of this many witnesses, Pepper. Catch your breath and trust me. Finally, our turn. Here we go."

Rush hour traffic gave me a fairly accurate gauge to spot any surveillance. When a tail's patience is stretched by other motorists cutting them off, going slow in the fast lane, or fluctuating in their speeds, the driver becomes enraged, impatient, and commits reckless errors that make them stand out. I didn't spot anyone tailing us—in front, behind, or on the sides.

Pepper was beginning to hyperventilate. Beads of nervous perspiration moistened her forehead.

"Breathe using your whole body," I told her.

"Fuck you."

Swerving over to the far right lane, I took the I-205 South exit.

I sealed my lips in frustration. I fought the urge to offer Pepper a gesture of comfort—a hand on her thigh, or even just a gentle caress on her cheek. She deserved to be protected, not to be sexed up.

In my peripheral vision, Pepper was stripping the tattered blouse off. Underneath she had on a silver camisole which her sweat had rendered see-through. I could discern the darker shade of her aureola beneath.

She caught me looking. Her lips flashed a dirty grin. "Enjoying the peep show, Matt?"

"We need to stop someplace to get you some clothes," I said. "Maybe a few groceries, too."

Pushing back into the seat, Pepper leveraged both feet up on the dash, stretching, her legs tight together. The curves and hollows of her abdomen flexed. Taking a deep breath, she engaged her core and bent forward until she could wrap her fingers around her ankles. She held for ten seconds, then went for another rep.

I edged into the right lane and drove slow, alternating between watching the road and Pepper's limber joints. I remembered grasping her ankle to push her left leg up and over until her toes tapped the headboard. It made for deeper penetration.

At the end of the tenth rep, Pepper regarded me with a cool, sultry gaze. "You're thinking about our fuck earlier, huh." The anger and stress in her voice had faded. "It's alright to want me, Matt. Maybe after this case we'll see each other again. Just don't expect us to remain exclusive. Because I know we're driven through life by our career choices."

"Listen to me, Pepper. You were in a vulnerable position last night, and whether you gave me permission or not doesn't change the fact that I made a mistake. I'm sorry."

Pepper removed her feet from the dash, and leaned back against the headrest. Her lips parted slightly in awe. "What did you come back to the parlor for?" she asked.

"I need your help. Did you open a file to catalogue a billing address or credit info toward a deposit for a skinhead Reggie eighty-sixed yesterday?"

"That piece o' shit didn't have the balls to kill her," Pepper said.

"Skinheads can run together like a pack of wolves. One of his fellow gang members could've paid the shop a visit while you were out shopping. Are you up for telling me how Dee-Dee was killed? Shot, strangled, stabbed—"

Pepper clamped a hand over her mouth, smacking the arm rest. She couldn't find the switch. Her cheeks swelled up and her eyes widened with nausea.

"Christ," I said, mashing the passenger window button on my console down.

Shoving her head out through the window, Pepper spewed vomit. The stream spattered the backseat window, a Jackson Pollack of green and yellow chunks across the glass. Velocity smeared the puke into a child's finger painting.

She flopped back into the seat, trying to catch her breath again. She lost it. The flood gates opened and she bawled.

I reached my right arm out. "I'm sorry, Pepper. Come here. It's going to be okay."

Sliding over, she nuzzled against my shoulder, sobs rattling her body.

"That's it," I said. "Let it out."

I sped through the yellow light at Eighty-Second and Johnson Creek to turn into Fred Meyer. Pulling around the lot, I got behind the last car in one of the lines at the gas station. The odor of gasoline sustained my heartache for Pepper's grief. I squeezed her shuddering form tighter against mine.

The attendant took my credit card poker-faced, acting like he didn't notice the half-naked chick cuddled up against me. "Fill the tank," I told him, keeping my voice low and conciliatory.

"Yes, sir."

We sat in a soothing calm until the gas jockey returned with the receipt.

"Is the women's restroom kept clean?" I asked.

"Yup, sure is."

"Get me the key for it, please."

Pepper rummaged through spare clothing I kept packed in a gym bag. While she was changing, I reached over and got into the glove box, then slammed the compartment shut. She came out of the bathroom a rock ballad on the radio later, wearing a pair of Leslie's flip-flops, my jeans cinched tight around her waist with the leg bottoms rolled up about four times, and a baggy PSU hoodie.

We sauntered into the one-stop shopping center through the sliding entrance. Compensating for the weight added to my step, I hoped no one noticed my slight foot drag.

Pepper waved playfully at a little boy on a purple dinosaur kiddy ride. A security guard observed us suspiciously from a discreet distance. Pepper tossed clothes, sandals, a few cosmetics, and packages of vegan-friendly food into a basket I lugged around for her. I paid with cash through the U-Scan checkout aisle.

We made another stop at the restrooms. While she took her time to change, I recalled a guy had been stabbed to death in the men's room a few years ago. I exhaled a sigh of relief when Pepper emerged dressed down in Columbia Sportswear sweatpants and a red tank top with a large black rose outlined on the lower right side.

Returning to the car, I opened the passenger side door for her.

"Where are you taking me now?" Pepper said.

"My office. Maybe there you'll feel secure enough to help me find a way to draw out Dee-Dee's killer."

EIGHT

Leslie Crow

THE SPEAKER that resembled a rock in the concrete planter by the front door to the Green Beans Coffee and Tea shop blared out reggae. I almost couldn't hear the bell jingle at my entrance. The tantalizing aroma of cinnamon and java made me feel warm and welcome. I walked up to the counter between the row of bussed tables that smelled faintly of grapefruit, and a refinished hutch next to the basement entrance. I tilted a look down there and didn't see any last-minute patrons hanging out.

Still a little shaky after the trouble out at Dee's ranch, I helped myself to a bottle of juice from the upright cooler by the walkway that led to the kitchen. Elegant permanent marker lettering on a pumpkin next to the cash register read: *Try A Pumpkin Pie Latte.* The polished steel of the espresso machine gleamed.

I saw Alexi at the sink by the back door bopping her shoulders and swinging her slender hips, up to her elbows in dishwater. Long and layered ash blonde locks with platinum highlights swayed to the rhythm of the music. Alexi's elfin, lush body filled out a tight charcoal tank and shredded gray jeans; I glimpsed scarlet bra straps. She was singing along with

Damian Marley as he insisted that a person's body, as a vessel for their soul, must not be judged by beauty alone.

The lyrics summed up Alexi's faith and belief in wearing her tattoos. Skeptical friends and disgusted relatives gave her shit all the time about the memorial tats she wore proudly being tantamount to self-mutilation or an admission of guilt. Alexi just wanted to keep the memories of her loved ones close to her.

I'd met Alexi two years ago. She'd moved to Washington from Oklahoma for her son to be closer to his dad. The price of the house Alexi bought was a bargain due to a rise of crime in the neighborhood. To keep her boy safe, Alexi set out to hire a security company to install an alarm system. Her first choice, a larger, well-known central station, sent a corporate prick to perform the threat assessment; he tried picking Alexi up by making sexual innuendos about her tattoos.

While perusing the classifieds in the *Oregonian* for a coffee shop business to buy, Alexi saw our ad for Alternative Investigations. The skull and filigree design of our logo, which resembled a back piece tattoo, appealed to her. Our focus on kick-starting what needed to be done to ensure her safety won her over. Alexi confided that she'd also gone with our referral because Digital Domain, a local security company, had been formed by Rachel Houston, a Gulf War vet. Alexi would've done almost anything to support a soldier.

I heard a rattle as she placed a plate on the rack to dry. Smacking the water faucet valve off, Alexi grabbed a towel and wiped a froth of suds off her hands and arms, uncovering a Purple Heart service medal tat on the underside of her right forearm. It was for a soldier she'd broken up with after his fourth deployment to Iraq. Circumstances led Alexi to believe he'd been shot and killed following the break up.

"We're closed," Alexi shouted out. "No more free coffee."

She mistook me for a transient whom she'd treated to a cup of Joe once. He'd started loitering four or five times every other day for another handout.

"What about to friends in need of a little refuge?" I yelled above the calypso beat that was rattling the mugs on the shelves opposite the espresso machine.

"Leslie! What's up, girlfriend?"

Walking up to the register, she took a remote out of her back pocket and turned down the volume. Making fists with our right hands, we bumped our knuckles together.

"Oh, just the usual," I said, giving Alexi a head bob. "Skip tracing, process serving, background checks. How are you?"

"Working my tail off. One of my baristas is on vacation, the other's attending Portland State and only covers weekends. Other than that, awesome," she said. "Mikey's turning seven next week. I'm planning a big sleepover. Lots of *Rock Hero*. Movies. A chocolate sheet cake from Costco."

"Mikey will love that," I said, allowing a sincere grin to tug up the corner of my mouth. "But what are *you* going to do to celebrate seven years as a mom?"

Beaming, Alexi reached into her other back pocket and yanked out a folded piece of sketchbook paper. She opened it carefully, as if it contained a fragile pressed flower, then placed it on the counter.

My eyes widened. It was a full-color portrait of her son. The artist had captured the happiness of his innocent gaze in brilliant detail. Reading the note beneath the tribute, I forgot to draw air into my lungs.

I can still add an inscription, but it won't be any stronger than his tattoo on your right arm. - Dee

The Celtic love knot in a green wooden frame hung by a string from a thumbtack on the top of her right forearm. Inscribed *Mother's Love*, it promised protection to her son.

"I've got an appointment in a couple of weeks," Alexi said. "She's going to ink him on my ribcage below my left breast. Hey, you okay?"

I gasped to breathe. *Oh Christ*, I thought, *she doesn't know.* That told me the media was still keeping the reports of Dee's murder buried. Rubbing the tear ducts in my eyes to keep the moisture back, I cleared my throat. "Yeah, I'm just whipped," I said. "Thanks. I dropped by to see if I could borrow the basement, stay the night. Maybe sort some shit out, line up a few motives and suspects in a high-profile case I'm working on."

"You know I loan out my space to friends whenever they need some solitude," Alexi said. "But isn't your office better equipped for that stuff?"

I considered dropping by the office for a second. That meant running into Matt. He'd try and talk me out of working the case, or second-guess my every move. Fuck that. Wiggling the strap of my laptop bag I said, "All the access and files I need are right here in my MacBook."

"Sounds razor," she said. "Where's Matt, though? He's got your back, doesn't he?"

"Yeah, he does," I told her. "There are aspects of this case that are personal, though, and I need to see them through by myself."

"Okay, sweetie." Alexi rubbed my shoulder. "The spare key's in the register. Just slip it through the front door mail slot when you're done. If I don't see it tomorrow, I'll call you."

"Thank you, Alexi."

"Don't thank me yet," she said with a carefree chuckle. "Help me dry the rest of these dishes. I'm running late and it's pizza night."

Mikey's favorite, I remembered. As I caught the dish towel Alexi threw at my head, I envisioned Dee hunched over her drawing board, pouring her soul and talent into that sketch of Alexi's boy. I almost didn't hear what she asked me next.

"So what's this huge case you're working on? Maybe talking about it in broad strokes will help you see the bigger details. You know how good a sounding board I am, and what's said in my coffee shop, stays in my coffee shop."

Tossing the towel aside, I rubbed my eyes as if I'd just chopped up an onion without running cold water. I still managed to keep the floodgates of my grief sealed. This wasn't the time or the place. I let my hands fall away, then delivered the bad news to her face.

"Dee's dead, Alexi," I told her, my voice choking up. "She was . . . murdered. I'm sorry."

"What? No way. You're putting me on."

I met her denial with a dread-filled gaze.

Slowly, the ice wall that kept her emotions sealed cracked right down the middle. Tears leaked through, streaking her cheeks in a crying jag. She dropped the blue mug she'd been drying and I heard it smash into pieces.

"Why would someone wanna kill her?" blubbered Alexi.

"That's what I'm going to find out," I said.

Leaning back against the edge of the sink for support, Alexi covered her face with both hands and wept louder. I slouched across from her, my head bowed. Sorrow boiled underneath every tattoo Dee had inked onto my skin.

•

BREATHING IN the aromatic steam rising from the cups of strong Earl Gray tea calmed our nerves. After Alexi tossed her wads of tear-soiled tissue into the trash, I explained that out of respect for our friendship and our status in Portland's tattoo community, I'd confided in her about Dee's demise; however, she needed to keep it quiet. Spreading the word could jeopardize the investigation, or even put her life at risk.

Alexi nodded, wrapped her hands around the cup. The heat absorbed the shock and diminished the trembling of her shoulders. "All I can think about right now is that she'll never be able to do my tattoo. Christ, that's really selfish, huh?" she whimpered, then snatched another Kleenex to dab her red eyes.

I reached across the table and rubbed her left shoulder. A ribbon banner at the top of her biceps streamed *Hopeless Romantic*. Inches below it, a skeleton grinning ear-to-ear in a blue blouse clutched a stainless steel, riveted, heart-shaped box with an anatomically-correct heart inside. "No," I said, "no, it doesn't. Are you okay to drive home?"

"Yeah, sure."

I walked Alexi to her jeep in the back lot, gave her a wave good night, then trotted back down the steps to the rear entrance.

After bolting the entrances, I swept up the pieces of the mug Alexi had dropped. Then I raided the fridge to build a veggie sandwich on a whole wheat bagel smeared with black bean hummus.

"Out of avocado . . . shit."

Balancing my dinner in one hand, the bottle of juice in the other, I moved into the low-ceilinged basement. My footsteps stamped across the cracked, lime green concrete floor. I didn't have to walk as quietly here as I did above my neighbors on the hardwood floors in my loft. I set my food and computer bag down on the large, round birch table to the left of the archway and snatched an issue of the *Portland Mercury* from one of the metal stands nearby, tossing it down beside my meal.

I plopped down onto one of the ladder-backed dining room chairs and perused the newspaper of Portland's alternative and weird culture in between nibbles of my sandwich. Some local metal bands touring through the Crystal Ballroom or Dante's piqued my interest. I thumbed the performance dates into my iPhone.

Advocates for the Eastmoreland and Sellwood neighborhood associations were rallying to block a vegan strip club from transforming Southeast McLoughlin into a red light district. They didn't want too many strip clubs giving the community a sex trade reputation or an increase in crime. I chuckled at that bullshit. Half a dozen strip clubs already thrived on that thoroughfare.

A full-page layout made me stop chewing. It was an advertisement for a tattoo convention at the Overseer Hotel downtown, starting tonight. The lurid designs and provocative, bikini-clad models on the spread didn't get my attention; the partial list of artists and shops that would be in attendance at the regional event did.

Despite the lump that formed in my throat, I managed to swallow my last bite. I recognized a name in ink lore I hadn't seen since my teenage years with Dee in San Francisco.

Daniil Sokolov, her tattoo mentor.

I remembered the first time Dee introduced me to him. Tattoo machine buzzing, he was inking Bruce Lee on a stuntman's massive biceps. Dan wore his long, scraggly brown hair in a tight ponytail. His thick, gray-frosted mustache was immaculately groomed. His body was lean and toned from having served in the Coast Guard, and frequent surfing. I'd also smelled baking clay, because his tattoo parlor doubled as a head shop where he sold clay ashtrays, bowls, and vases he spun and hand-glazed.

I fondly recalled the lesson in linguistics Dan gave me when he taught me the correct pronunciation of his name. His surname meant "falcon." He was proud that his identity matched one of his hobbies.

He adored birds. One of his favorite pastimes was sitting in parks and, in between tossing handfuls of bread crumbs or seed, watching birds splashing in birdbaths, and sketching them. Later, those designs would grace his pottery—or, if he felt a patron was worthy enough, a tattoo.

The phoenix Dee had inked on my abs was inspired by one of Dan's drawings.

These fragments I'd managed to retain seemed like another lifetime ago. Intrigued that I still remembered so much about this man, I set up my MacBook, then Googled his name. It dawned on me that taking this detour may have been an unnecessary distraction, or even worse, lead to more heartache, but maybe my friend wasn't killed for something she did or saw.

Scars on my body I'd endured while investigating my mom's murder on the rez in South Dakota reminded me every day how hazardous a family heritage can be.

Fingers scrolling and clicking from page to page, I viewed blogs and news bites that filled a few gaps in the last twenty years. In the early nineties Dan had refused to tattoo a famous rap artist because his lyrics ridiculed homosexuality. Later in the decade he assisted a deputy DA in identifying a number of Russian and Ukrainian mobsters by their tattoos.

The latest article I skimmed made me feel grim. A blogger lamented that sightings of Dan's work and tattoo celebrity had become scarce. He surmised that either Dan had entered witness protection after testifying against the criminal underworld, or the demise of several of his friends in the gay community from AIDS had finally taken a toll, and driven Dan into a self-imposed exile of mourning.

The skin of my back pulsating again with a dull ache irritable enough to want to scratch, I clutched my go-bag instead and rushed for the bathroom. As I stretched to rub aftercare cream in hard to reach places, my shoulders popped.

NINE

Matt Grudge

ONE ARM wrapped tightly around Pepper's narrow waist, I kept my other hand loose, ready for a defensive move if someone made another attempt to nab her. We were walking fast toward the northeast corner of Fifth and Morrison. I panned a keen gaze along the Nike Portland showroom floor windows. Streetlights gleaming off of the silver mannequins posed in hurdles and sprints would illuminate a stalker's reflection as well.

Across the street, uniformed security guards were locking the northwest entrance to Pioneer Place. A couple on their way out of the mall toting an assortment of bags and boxes tossed a few dollars into a street musician's instrument case. Leaning back against a signpost, the alto sax player blew out a smooth nocturne. The eclectic architecture of downtown's business and retail district threw back echoes of the deep notes.

At the corner I steered us right. Strong winds from an approaching storm whipped along the corridor. The gusts sweeping around the crevices of nearby buildings made eerie siren music. I smelled BO and fast food grease.

Pepper's hood blew off her head, startling her as cold air hit her exposed face. Some suit blocking the doors to the Kress Building, a Bluetooth pressed to his ear and his overcoat flapping in the wind, took notice. I decided he was just an innocent bystander stunned by Pepper's gorgeous looks, and not a lookout, and elbowed him aside, growling, "Get out of the way." I wrenched the door open.

"Fuck you, punk," he yelled in Russian-accented English, the closing glass door muffling his aggravation.

The white and gold town clock mounted above the elevator read 9:15 p.m. Dee-Dee's murder had taken place more than twenty-four hours ago. The killers could be long gone by now. The possibilities of obtaining any hard leads were fading. My gut tightened at the pressure of the time crunch as I made a beeline across the elegant lobby for the elevator embedded in the black and green marble wall.

Pepper dragged her feet a little, breathing in marathon bursts of air. "Ease up, Matt," she said, wriggling out of my grip. "Where the hell are you taking me?"

Smacking the call button with my palm, I glanced up at the digital display as it counted down from the top floor to four. A few seconds later it lit up on three and didn't change. The delay upped my pulse. I nudged the door to the left open with my hip. "My office," I said, yanking Pepper by her arm into the fire stairwell.

"You've gotta be fucking with me," she said.

Her voice reverberated up the stairwell and our stomping footsteps beat a stressful ostinato on the metal steps. Surging with adrenaline, I barely felt the burn in my thighs, and I nearly led us past the second floor door. Bringing us to an abrupt halt, I backpedaled, then cracked the door for the second floor open. I watched a janitor wearing earbuds wiping off one of the glass office doors. The pane squeaked.

"Don't be a cocky asshole, Matt," she whispered. "You really expect me to believe that a pair of low-rent investigators work out of a building listed on the National Register of Historic Places?"

"Why not?" I whispered back through the side of my mouth. "It's nondescript. There are plenty of other businesses here my clients can name if they need to deny seeing me."

The elevator dinged, the doors parted, and the janitor wheeled their jumbo-sized garbage can inside. The door slid shut and the floor indicator flashed to five. "Okay," I said. "All clear. Stay close."

We darted out of the stairwell and walked rapidly past the elevator and down the hallway. Stopping at the last door on the left, I unlocked the doorknob and deadbolt, pushed the door open, and nodded for Pepper to get inside. I followed right behind her, turning to shut and double-lock the door again. Flipping on the lights for the outer office and waiting area, I grimaced as I always did, revealing my place to someone I hoped to inspire confidence in me. The interior hadn't been remodeled since the seventies and made me feel like I was welcoming clients to step into a time machine. Fortunately, the wooden fixtures and the swank, sixties-style bachelor pad furniture Leslie had scrounged up at garage sales and head shops on Hawthorne gave our digs a retro vibe.

Most people warmed up to the environment. Pepper winced with disgust. Walking to the center of the room, she panned a glance at Leslie's thrashed desk on the left, then down at the davenport that faced the wall by the door, where my and Leslie's framed state certificates to operate as private investigators hung close together. Back issues of loss prevention, firearm, and tattoo aficionado magazines littered the round-legged cherrywood coffee table in front of the leather couch. "Maybe you should dust off your expense account, Matt, and put us up for the night in a cheap motel somewhere."

"Why?" I said. "What's wrong?"

"If you think I'm sleeping on a slab fitted with a cow that had a face," Pepper said, "you're hugely mistaken."

"I'll take the couch. There's a hammock in my office. Come on, I'll give you the nickel tour." I left out explaining that if anyone tried to break in and abduct her, they'd have to get by me first.

As she followed me through the foyer between the two rooms, I pushed the bathroom door to the right open. "There's a shower in there," I said. "It might relax you."

"Yeah, sure. I'm supposed to be at a tattoo convention. Some clients are going to be really pissed when I don't show up to do their ink. When word of that gets around to my competitors, the rumor mill will grind my reputation into dust."

Before opening the door to my office, I turned to face her. "Don't be so hard on yourself, Pepper," I said earnestly. "Your clients will understand."

"What am I supposed to tell them?" she said, her voice rising, becoming shrill. "Sorry I blew off your appointment. I had to hide from a psychopath that killed my boss. And since Dee's murder wasn't reported anywhere in the media, I'd be better off blowing them off like a geek in high school asking me out—by telling them I had to wash my goddamn hair."

"If you're through feeling sorry for yourself," I said, "there's something in here I could use your help with."

"Fuck you, Matt."

Throwing the door to my office open, I clutched Pepper's elbow and muscled her across the threshold.

"Let me go," she said, trying to pull away and succeeding only in stretching the sleeve of her hooded sweatshirt.

I released her in case I needed to defend myself if she became as violent as she had earlier. Striding over to my cluttered desk, I tilted the positional lamp around and switched it on. It cast a brilliant spotlight on a huge dry-erase board.

Pepper squinted, bewildered by the data scribbled on the white surface and plastered with sticky notes of assorted colors and photographs affixed with magnets. I dug the laser pointer keychain from my jacket pocket and wiggled the red dot at a section headlined by Dee-Dee's name and a grainy photograph of the slain tattoo artist I'd clipped out of a newspaper in a recycle bin.

"What the hell is this?" she asked.

"Outlines of active cases," I told her. "And as you can see, this section for Dee is a void. Maybe you can help me fill it in. Tell me anything, no matter how dull or simple it sounds."

I uncapped a black marker with my teeth. The pungent odor gave me a buzz. Breathing through my mouth, I drew a horizontal line above yesterday's date, then added a few vertical dashes spaced apart for time markings. "When did you return from Food Fight?" I asked around the cap in my mouth, peering over my shoulder at Pepper. Observing her body language would alert me to any fabrications.

Pepper tugged the sweatshirt up off her body, revealing a low-cut tank and skin beaded with perspiration. Taking a deep breath, she pulled one of the two chairs facing my desk around. She plopped down in it, then rubbed her forehead as if trying to relieve a migraine.

"Yesterday afternoon was booked solid with clients," she began. "I finished coloring the bust of Bettie Page on a stripper's biceps a little after three. The customer at four only needed a banner added, so Dee took that appointment over and told me to go to the store. I walked. While I was visiting with Chad as he rang up my groceries, Dee called my cell and reminded me to get an item I'd almost forgotten . . . Oh shit, what the fuck was it?"

"Tell me more about the four o'clock appointment," I said. Maybe they'd fled from the studio after witnessing the murder.

"No show. Dee was angry because they flaked out, called her five minutes late and confessed to getting their tat done elsewhere for less money. Unappreciative asshole. You start a tattoo with an artist, you finish it with that artist."

"Did you get a receipt at Food Fight?" I asked.

"Yes. It's back at the studio, though."

The solvent odor from the marker was beginning to make me feel lightheaded. Removing the cap from my mouth, I went to click it in place over the felt tip when my hands trembled, and I stroked a slash of ink across my knuckle. Another reason for Pepper's headache and my sudden outbreak of the shakes dawned on me. "When's the last time you ate?"

"Late breakfast of vanilla soy yogurt sprinkled with granola around eleven," Pepper said. "Why?"

"We're crashing," I told her, capping the pen and setting it down on the shelf below the board. "Let's make some food." I reached around Pepper to grab the brown bag of groceries she'd placed on my desk before taking a seat.

Rubbing her temples with both hands, she peered up at me imploringly. "How do you expect me to eat, Matt, when you're treating me like a suspect?"

"I wouldn't be helping you prove an alibi otherwise," I said, riffling through the contents. "What do we have here? A bag of arugula and shredded carrots. Microwavable brown rice. Green onions. Bell peppers. Jar of minced garlic." I held up a package that contained a pair of small bricks that resembled firm sponges stained a dark, golden tan. "What's this stuff?"

"Teriyaki marinated tofu." Pepper rose, took the vegan staple out of my fingers, and dropped it back in the bag. "Since you fixed dinner this morning," she said, "it's only fair I make it tonight. Do you have a hot plate? A skillet? Maybe some utensils?"

She took the bag of groceries out of my hands and cradled it in the crook of her arm. The subtle move accentuated her bosom. She walked away from the desk in search for cooking utensils, her walk deliberate enough to taunt me with her figure, but slow with exhaustion.

"Hold it," I said. "Stay away from the windows. All the stuff we need is in a cabinet behind Leslie's desk."

I walked back to the outer office. The flip-flops on Pepper's feet snapped behind me. As I shifted and banged things around to gather the cookware, she knelt at the coffee table across from the couch. Leafing through a magazine, she sniffed the air. "Why do I smell mint?"

"Toothpaste," I said, shoving the periodicals aside to set the hot plate down. "We used some as spackle to fill in a couple bullet holes. Like you said, Pepper, we're low-rent."

"Matt, I didn't mean it like that."

I sat down on the mocha shag carpet beside her. "Sure you did. It's okay. I can take it. Actually, I wouldn't prefer it any other way."

"What do you mean?" Pepper asked.

"Under my piercings and tats, killers don't see a third-generation investigator with over a decade's worth of experience on their trail," I said. "And if my ruse doesn't nail them, I'm not afraid to make something happen." I offered her a small cutting board and a fillet knife to slice and dice the veggies. My hands didn't shake now.

"Jesus, Matt." Her lip quivered. "You sound suicidal." Pepper snatched the rubber board and the blade, then pushed to her feet.

"No," I said, "just *underestimated*."

Moments later I heard the tap running at the bathroom sink, then the knife hitting the cutting board. I dug my cell phone out of my pocket and flipped it open. I keyed in the password, then scrolled down several missed calls and voice messages. None from Leslie. Three from Derek Sharp. What did that bottom feeder want? Persistent little shit had even sent me an incomplete text with a hyperlink to his blog.

Check out these photos. There's an important—

Since the handset didn't have Internet access, I went to my desk to retrieve my laptop, walking by the bathroom. Rapid movements caught my eye. Pepper was deftly cutting up the veggies with an ease that was intriguing to watch.

After rinsing the bell pepper thoroughly, she tossed it upward. Tendrils of water spattered her hair and cheeks. Swiftly, she raised the tip of the fillet knife. Gravity skewered the vegetable. Gently holding the base of the pepper, she carved around the stem. Twirling the handle between her fingers to move the blade aside, she scooped out the seeds with the index finger and thumb of the same hand, then quartered and rapidly chopped the pepper on the board.

"Where did you learn how to handle a knife like that?"

"Practice," she said, rinsing the steel off.

On late-night infomercials or culinary reality shows, I'd seen chefs prepare food with a similar flair. Pepper's precision leaned more toward a survivalist in the wild. I remembered the brief story about her backpacking excursion to Romania. I wondered what other skill sets she'd developed in that wooded and mountainous terrain of dark legends. I remembered Reggie's warning: *"She isn't the same girl ever since returning from Europe."*

"What are you staring at?" Pepper said.

"Nothing," I assured her, moving on to my office.

Silver laptop tucked under my arm, power cord and adapter clenched in my fist, I returned to set the computer up on the coffee table away from the hot plate and cast-iron skillet radiating warmth. While I waited for the laptop to boot up, Pepper came out and dumped veggies into the pan to sizzle. She spread the chunks around the searing surface evenly with a wooden spoon.

"Here's some olive oil," I said, offering her a clear squeeze bottle.

"No," she said. "Vegetables have their own juices."

Selecting the home link for Sharp's blog, I watched the security bar integrated into the web navigation software closely for any spyware or viruses detected.

Female porn stars in heavy makeup, dressed up as executive assistants or anachronistic gumshoes in trench coats and snap-brim fedoras, gazed sensually from the masthead and borders. The open folds of their attire revealed black-stockinged stems and perfectly-rounded curves that'd either been air-brushed or a plastic surgeon's procedure. The articles I skimmed, played up with pulp-style prose, spun crime and tragedy into sensationalized gossip. Comments posted by his subscribers were hasty, ignorant, misspelled, or laden with acronyms—contributors to the death of the English language.

Overall, the site's disingenuous presentation added layers of facade damaging or distracting to a private investigator's trade. I knew police officers and detectives in law enforcement criticized Leslie and me in a similar fashion. The fact was, our body modifications and thrashed clothes were simply a lifestyle change.

Pepper added the carrots, stirred to combine them, and turned down the hot plate's heat before kneeling beside me to peer over my shoulder at the laptop screen. Her breath teased my inner ear, raised my body temperature. "Are we surfing for porn?"

"This is the blog of a local scam artist that tries to sell himself as a true-crime reporter," I told her. "All afternoon he's been nagging me that he's found a lead in Dee-Dee's murder."

"Shit," Pepper said, "really?"

Satisfied that the antivirus software had not detected anything by now, I typed in the link Sharp had sent. "Don't get your hopes up," I warned. "This prick deals in hype."

Two hi-res photographs almost filled the screen. The first picture, date stamped around a year ago, showed a man with a crew cut and a cruel mouth, wearing a navy blue nylon jacket. In his hands he displayed an AK-47. Behind him another guy wearing an identical jacket swung an axe into an armoire of aged wood. The sharp focus captured splinters flying. I made out the bold yellow letters on the axe man's coat: ATF.

A lady behind the agents with mascara running down her high cheekbones was screaming in a rage, both hands pressed against her temples. A tailored, medium-length red skirt suit wrapped her ballet dancer's figure, and high heels strapped around the ankles drew attention to her firm legs. Manicured fingers crammed with glittery bling were plunged into her mane of albino hair, loosening a few strands from a tight bun.

The caption beneath the photo read: *Contraband Weapons Seized At Ukrainian Gangster's Estate Sale.*

Only half of the second picture downloaded. A gunmetal gray sky swirled over a portion of downtown's skyline, backdrop for an array of people's heads in the foreground. No date stamp. My instincts didn't need a tag to figure out where and when the photograph had been taken. I'd been there just yesterday.

Sharp had snapped a shot of the reporters and looky-loos gathered around the entrance to Femme Ink. The clouds didn't look as dark as when we'd been there, so I estimated it was taken before Leslie and I had arrived. Nothing else in the partial image provided a lead. The backs of heads taunted me, and I felt anger flush my entire face. I almost shouted at the coifed brunette, the red-headed bob, the ash blonde curls caught up in an ornate butterfly clip, and the salt-and-pepper ponytail, but I managed to contain my ire.

I heard a pop as a jar lid twisted open, then caught a whiff of garlic. With an exhausted sigh, I said, "Well, I don't see anything urgent in these photos. Do you?" I pivoted around to gauge Pepper's reaction as she added half a teaspoon of the minced garlic to the concoction.

"No," she said hesitantly and blinked. Her brows, punctuated by silver and gold loops, had been lifted with shock a second earlier.

"Don't lie to me, Pepper."

"Look at the albino in the red suit and the blonde in the lineup again," she told me. "The rings on her fingers obscure it in the first picture, but they're wearing the same hair clip. It looks antique or handmade. Then again, it could just be a coincidence."

I closed the laptop. "Which fits Derek Sharp's MO to a T. He throws out these vague clues, the wrong clues, wasting time. Next time I see him, I'm gonna stomp on him like a—that sure smells terrific." I nodded at the skillet. "Another dish you learned how to make in Romania? I don't recall you being vegan when we first met."

"A few weeks into the hike, our meat supply ran out. So we lived mostly on vegetables and some grains, fruits, and nuts donated by farmers. I hope you like garlic. I'll always appreciate it for repelling mosquitoes."

After we ate dinner and hashed out some good memories, Pepper excused herself. As I listened to the spray of water from the bathroom, relieved she felt comfortable enough to take a shower, I realized the problem about the uploads that aroused my suspicions: Sharp's latest message and photos had been interrupted.

I shrugged. It was probably just a server error. I went to my office for a tin of mints. The crisp wintergreen flavor cut through the garlic odor on my breath. Reclining in my chair, I propped my sneakers up on the desk, then sent the instant message to Leslie's MacBook before redialing her cell number.

TEN

Leslie Crow

I RETURNED to the kitchen and washed my plate, then I finished drying and putting away the dishes, listening absently as the radio repeated the news report from the morning: gossip about the latest Hollywood scandal; the fall reality TV shows with the highest ratings; the announcement about Mayor Sam Adams and Governor John Kitzhaber attending a dinner tonight with dignitaries of the Russian government.

I flinched and almost dropped the last dish.

This minuscule detail in itself seemed insignificant, until I remembered the foreign letters printed on the shred of clothing I found in the burn barrel out at the ranch. I hustled back down to the table in the basement and yanked the plain paper bag in which I'd stashed the items from the ranch out of my computer bag. I dumped the contents onto the table, seeking the Baggie with the bullet inside. Holding it up to the floor lamp nearby, I studied it with a magnifying glass to read the caliber—only I couldn't, because the numerals were in a language I didn't know.

I did a Google search for "Russian numerals" for comparison, and pulled a pair of latex gloves—*snap . . . snap.*

Carefully, I unrolled the damp newspaper. Water-stained Cyrillic script widened my eyes and drove theories into my head like a railroad spike. Obviously, an international connection existed between the trespassers at Dee's place and the circumstances behind her death. I made a leap and wondered if Dee had been murdered by the mobsters her mentor had exposed as a means to bring him out into the open.

I needed more evidence. Unfolding the paper, I carefully peeled the cover page over. Halfway through the turn, a quarter-inch rip tore across the paper. "Shit."

I let it go to reach inside my go-bag. Plugging the portable hairdryer in, I switched it on low and waved the stream of air over the periodical. A little while later the pages were dry enough for me to peruse them for clues.

One of the newspaper's previous readers had marked it up thoroughly. I spotted words and lines of text circled, highlighted, or underlined. Notes in Cyrillic were even scrawled in some of the margins. On the back, next to a word find and a comic strip, I found a mailing label, but between the strike-throughs from a permanent marker and water damage, I couldn't make out the recipient's name or address.

Frustrated, I pressed my palms against my temples. After taking several deep breaths to release the tension, I picked up the thick, greeting card-sized envelope. Having been protected underneath the newspaper, it wasn't as rain-damaged. The stock felt expensive; luxurious, even. I untucked the flap and slid a card out.

In my hands I held an invitation to the Russian dinner at the Overseer Hotel.

A wicked idea curled my lip into a smirk. For a second, I entertained the thought of getting gussied up in a cocktail dress and high heels, or my skirt suit I wore at court appearances, to crash the diplomatic dinner. *For a second.* Even though I knew that I was capable of pulling a chameleon of that fashion for a political event, my pride kept me honest. *I'm a PI, not eye candy for a bunch of bureaucratic weasels.*

Returning to the newspaper, I focused on the annotated articles, running every word through a translation website for answers. The two hours this took to accomplish felt like two days.

I saw the instant message icon in the corner of the laptop display blinking like a heart monitor. The rapid beats increased my own pulse, wrecking the calm I'd started feeling. I positioned the pointer over the smiley face, then gave the mouse a perturbed click with my middle finger. The text that followed Matt's black and white icon read: *Answer your goddamn phone, please.*

My eyes narrowed in anger. I pulled my go-bag over. Ripping the side pocket zipper open, I found my iPhone and unlocked it with a thumb swipe. "What?"

"Where the hell have you been?" Matt's tone was urgent, borderline frantic. "I've been trying to reach you for hours."

"Why? Do you have something? Or are you just freaking out about the blood I'm going to spill hunting for the killer? Give me a break. I was following up a lead out at Dee's farm."

"I watched the ATM footage from the bank across the street," he said. "I e-mailed stills of a possible suspect to you. Did you see them? Christ, what's that smell?"

"No . . . I've been researching another angle. Tell me about the footage, Matt."

"A skinhead got thrown out for wanting a tattoo covered up. Maybe he returned."

I admired his resolve in acquiring the video. It proved that Matt was taking this case seriously, his PI trade deep in his bones. But his thin theory made me want to puke. "We could watch camera surveillance until our eyes bleed and make up a dozen suspects."

"You have a better suggestion?" Matt said. "Let's hear it."

"The media blackout suppressing Dee's murder proves that higher stakes are involved. An extreme right fascist doesn't warrant that thorough a cover-up. An international crime with locales and parties from all over the globe would."

Matt coughed and nearly choked. "So you really think Dee-Dee's murder has political ties."

He took a deep breath, released it slowly. It didn't sound as if he was trying to keep his frustration or temper in check, though; more like something was arousing him.

"Yes," I yelled. "Are you chatting with a Suicide Girl again? Pay attention—"

"Leslie, your friend was killed by a hold-up gone wrong, someone she pissed off, or maybe even for something she saw. This is Portland, not Washington, DC, bullshit."

"Bullshit? I had an encounter with a Russian goon at Dee's ranch. I found evidence of a shootout there, too. The man who taught Dee how to ink was a Russian immigrant, helped law officers identify members of the Russian mafia by their tats. And he's supposedly at the Overseer Hotel downtown right now for a tattoo convention. We need to ask him if he recalls anything about the mobsters his knowledge assisted in incarcerating."

"What's his name?"

"Daniil Sokolov," I told him, pronouncing it 'Dah-nee-l.'

He paused, writing it down, I hoped. "Dan Sokolov. Got it."

"No," I said. "Are you *listening* to me? If you call him Dan, he will blow you off. Dah-nee-l. Try dropping my name with your introduction. Maybe he'll remember me."

"Leslie, why don't you just come along?"

"I've got someone else to interview and he doesn't like you," I said.

"Who? Don't tell me that true-crime blogger, what's-his-name, tried to contact you, too."

"Derek Sharp? Why is that parasite still trying to leech information from us? I think I hit him too hard. Did he say anything that might be a real tip?"

"He said he'd be willing to trade information from another story that may be connected to Dee-Dee's murder," Matt told me. "Something to do with an ATF raid on an estate sale and destroying antiques to expose contraband weapons, or some bullshit."

"Yeah," I said, "and we're being featured in a loss prevention magazine next month as the Pacific Northwest's top private detectives."

Matt said "calm down" or "chill out," but I was getting too pissed off to listen clearly. I would've slugged him in the mouth if he was here.

"Very funny, Leslie. Top private detectives. I'm rolling on the floor here." Then, to someone else on his end he said, "Yes, next Saturday. Sure, I'd like to go see that—" Matt stopped talking abruptly, his silence as guilty as a kid reaching into a cookie jar before dinner.

You've got to be fucking kidding, I thought. *He's making a date.* "Who's that with you, Matt?" I said, setting my jaw.

He told me about hooking up with Pepper Rourke, Dee's manager of Femme Ink, to comfort her after the crime scene technicians finished collecting evidence. Matt's careful choice of words and the bravado in his tone told me he'd gotten laid. Reckless asshole. Pepper had to have been an A-1 suspect in the murder because she had complete access to the scene of the crime. I was also aware of their history. Grudgingly, I gave Matt the benefit of the doubt and hoped the risk he was taking was because he believed Pepper was a suspect too.

"Did she give you any clues before or after you fucked her?"

"We need to avoid a scandal that'll blemish tattoo culture," he said.

"No shit, Sherlock. So, you didn't get any useful leads out of Pepper? Did you at least look around the parlor, Dee's station, for something the cops might've missed?"

"She's here with me because of this case, Leslie. Someone knows I stayed the night . . ." He stopped and backtracked. "Someone knows she talked to me and after trying to kidnap Pepper, tore the parlor and studio apartment apart looking for a bug they believe I planted."

"Watch her close, Matt."

"You said that as if I'm making a mistake," he said. "I'm protecting a source. Nothing more."

"*Sure* you are. As sure as I am that Pepper's keeping you on a short leash with her pussy. Check in after you've—" He ended the connection before I finished saying, "talked to Daniil. Wear a condom."

Feeling the strain in my eyes from the glare of the screen's backlight, I closed my MacBook, then took a break to stretch. Martin Goldman preferred to work graveyard shifts at the morgue, which gave me just under two hours to wrap up sifting for data. The ME's name had been jotted down next to an article about the bodies of three teenage girls recovered from a church fire on Squaw Mountain in Estacada.

ELEVEN

Matt Grudge

WHILE LESLIE was ranting about the media blackout and a probable link to international espionage, the bathroom door opened. Steam escaped to drift up around the popcorn ceiling. Pepper emerged into the foyer, her voluptuous torso wrapped in a large white bath towel.

Peeking through the damp bangs of hair she'd colored ash blonde, Pepper caught me looking and stared back hypnotically, her brown eyes now a creamy shade of green.

I cleared a lump in my throat. "So you really think Dee-Dee's murder has political ties," I said to Leslie.

Pepper undulated over to the corner of my desk and snatched the other Freddy's bag full of clothes. The dim light from the banker's lamp illuminated the black and gray tattoos on her smooth alabaster thighs like shadows. Turning her back toward me, she briefly regarded the case board before untucking the towel to let it drop.

Drawing a deep breath, I leaned forward to take a good look at her enormous back piece, from the rounded shoulders to the tailbone. A pinup variation of the four-armed Hindu goddess Kali glared at me with shifty, exotic eyes. Shaking my head in awe, I managed to find my voice and told Leslie she was full of shit.

Facing the desk comfortably nude, Pepper dumped the contents of the sack on my calendar blotter, then flung the plastic at my lap. She selected a pair of bubblegum pink, lace-trimmed cotton panties and bit the sales tag off. After slipping them on over wide hips, she grabbed a black push-up bra and dangled it in front of my face before fitting the molded cups over her breasts, then reaching behind her back to clasp the hooks. Holding my eyes hostage with a molten gaze, she slowly and deliberately pulled the thin straps up over her shoulders.

Despite Leslie's voice being right up against my ear, her urgent arguments sounded as distant as a football coach yelling at his players over the cheers of spectators.

Until the name of a contact at the Overseer Hotel she dropped resonated loud and clear.

Pulling my feet off the desk, I sprang forward in the chair. I yanked the top drawer open, shuffled supplies around, pricked a finger on a thumbtack, but found a pad of Post-It notes.

As she bent forward to pull on a pair of black jeans, Pepper's cleavage lingered suggestively before me. Reaching blindly for a pen in the mug full of writing utensils near the edge of the desk, I knocked the cup over the side. In a fluid motion Pepper's hand shot downward, then placed the mug back on the desk.

"Dan Sokolov. Got it," I said in a distracted tone.

Leslie's temper blew. "No! Are you *listening* to me?"

I pulled the handset away from my ear.

Perching along the front of the desk, Pepper tilted the lampshade to throw more light on her body, which also lit up the board of active cases. Outlines ranged from background checks to tracking a greedy software programmer with a stripper fetish who'd abandoned his wife and daughter two years ago. Glaring at the work lists, she raised a leg up onto the tabletop, kicking out at the side of the board with the other. The wheels squeaked as the vertical surface rolled sideways out of sight.

After jotting down the correct pronunciation for the contact's name, I told Leslie about Derek Sharp and his lame offering of a lead. She dismissed it quickly with a snarky remark about our rep. Tilting my head to re-ignite eye contact with Pepper as she fastened the tiny buttons of a sheer, plum rayon sleeveless blouse that matched her fingernails, I refrained from insult.

"Take it easy," I said. "Very funny, Leslie. Top private detectives . . ."

Narrowing her gaze, Pepper snatched a movie schedule clipping from the blotter and held it up closer to her face, which grew excited as a geek's. I noticed that in addition to revamping her hair and eye color, she'd taken out the piercings in her lips, nose, and brows (also dyed blonde) and covered the holes evenly with a foundation that blended flawlessly with her skin tone. "Is this current?" she asked. "If it is, we're going. *North By Northwest* is my *favorite* Hitchcock flick."

"Yes, next Saturday. Sure, I'd like to go see that—"

"Who's that with you, Matt?" Leslie said, sounding eager for a fight.

I'd forgotten to press the phone against my shoulder. So much for revealing Pepper's presence at a more appropriate moment. "Pepper Rourke. After the crime scene techs finished processing the parlor last night, she needed company, so I dropped by and . . . interviewed her. Pepper discovered Dee-Dee's body and she's—"

The case board and the desk blotter whirled with the dark atmosphere of my office as Pepper spun my seat around. One hand on a jutting hip, Pepper removed the other from the back of the chair to trace a line up her abs, then between her boobs, to tap her chin with an index finger. "Is that what you call it? Maybe I should refresh your memory."

"She's trying to help me piece together some leads," I finished.

While Leslie and I argued about the clues I didn't discover, Pepper slid her flexible legs into the gaps between the armrests and the seat back, then snuggled across my lap to straddle my crotch. The chair creaked noisily and tilted backward a few inches. My penis hardened quickly in the warm closeness as her hips started grinding back and forth. It took every grain of discretion I possessed to keep from groaning her name over the phone. That and biting my lip.

I took another tack, assuring Leslie that Pepper was with me because my visit had placed her in danger. She needed protection.

"Watch her close, Matt," Leslie said, her tone exuding cynicism.

Annoyed at Leslie's comment that I was being a slave to pussy, I ended the call and tossed the handset on the desk.

"Oh, God," I moaned, straining to hold onto the climax building up in my groin every second Pepper rubbed up against my bulging cock. I groped her taut ass cheeks with both hands to pull her coital curves tighter against my genitals. Pepper unbuttoned her blouse and bra faster than she'd put them on and tossed the garments at the case board. The bra snagged a corner by the photograph of a stripper.

I took in Pepper's makeover and blurted a question that couldn't wait for our mutual pleasure. "What's with the disguise?"

"You're making me so wet. Mmmmm, unnnhhh. Use your hands more. Move your hands all over me. Yeah. Ohhh . . ."

Grasping her breast, I flicked my tongue at the nipple already engorged by the piercing through it. Pepper raked her nails along my scalp and moaned low. Feeling the stretch of her body through my clothes was pulling me away from motives and suspects with every breath, gasp, and wiggle.

I heard my wristwatch beep. Opening my eyes, I checked the time. Ten p.m. already. Shit! That left just two hours to make contact with Sokolov.

Pepper realized I'd stopped jerking my pelvis with her rhythm. She peered down at me askance as I let go of her tit and gently caressed the skin above her ribs, sliding my hand down to her waistline, then to trace her pierced belly button with my thumb.

"What the fuck, Matt?"

"You deserve better than this," I said.

"I'll nibble. What do you have in mind, stud?"

"Have you ever been to the Overseer Hotel?"

"That's where the tattoo convention I was supposed to attend is being held," Pepper said.

"Leslie's identified an artist there who might know something. After I meet with him, you and I can check into a room."

Snaking her arms around me in a hug, Pepper breathed into my ear, "But I want you inside me *now*."

I braced her backside with my forearms and rose from the chair, her calves tightening against the backs of my thighs for purchase. I set her feet on the floor and kissed her forehead before I moved over to the case board. Snatching her clothes, I tossed them over. "Get dressed."

Pepper donned the bra and buttoned the blouse back up, leaving the top three buttons undone to flaunt her amazing bust, then stomped into the bathroom for her purse. As I switched off the lights, she walked by me out the door and said, "Now I remember what a *dick* you can be when you're working."

●

RAIN DOUSED the windshield in a deluge as I turned into the nighttime parking area for Powell's City of Books on Northwest Tenth Street. I reached into the backseat to grab a wooden beach umbrella. For a second I imagined a sandy coastline extending to the blue ocean surf, a book opened in my hands, Pepper stretched out on an oversized towel, sunning her back with the bikini top untied to avoid tan lines. A boom of thunder brought me back to reality.

Unfurling the green umbrella as I stepped out into the downpour, I moved around to the passenger side to keep Pepper covered and dry. Huddled together, we walked west up Burnside and passed the entrance to Portland's biggest independent bookstore. A transient in a trash bag poncho, his salt-and-pepper hair stringy with rain under a corduroy baseball cap, bellowed from the curb, "*Street Roots*. Get your *Street Roots*," offering the newspaper about downtown's homeless community and culture.

The main thoroughfare that separated Portland's east and west sides was jammed with pedestrians and automobiles, especially at this hour on a Thursday night. One block farther up in the illustrious Pearl District, we approached the busy turn-in entrance for the Overseer Hotel.

An eyesore of modern architecture, the twenty-storey skyscraper occupied property that once belonged to a brewery landmark. According to word on the street, the Overseer almost didn't get built, but city lawmakers buckled when the construction firm incorporated clean technology and organic design to benefit sustainability and promote unity between urban commerce and the natural environment.

Closing the umbrella, I followed Pepper through the tinted slider doors into the lobby, an eclectic spread of maple totems, timber lodge decor, an arboretum, and a backdrop of surreal, biomechanical artwork. A medium-sized cauldron full of umbrellas sat just inside the entrance. I stuffed mine in there and jogged to catch up with Pepper as she sashayed toward the registration desk.

"Would you please help me get a message to Dah-nee-l Sokolov," I said to the brunette receptionist with a white orchid tucked above her ear.

After tapping the keyboard set inside the counter she said, "We have a Dan Sokolov registered, but no 'Dah-nee-l.' Sorry."

"He's a Russian tattoo artist up from San Francisco for the convention. By saying his full name *phonetically*," I said by way of explanation, "he'll know it's important. My name's Matt Grudge. Tell him Leslie Crow sent me. I'll be at the bar for as long as it takes."

Rolling her eyes as if I were just another crank, the receptionist did as I asked. After placing the call to Sokolov's room she gave me a forced grin. "I left a message and I'll overhead page him in a little while. The lounge is that way. It closes at two a.m. For non-registered guests there is a ten dollar drink minimum per hour, per person."

The lounge resembled a Scottish pub with its wooden paneling and the selection of fifty beers served in Imperial pint glasses. My kind of joint, except for the prices.

Hunkered down on a stool at the bar, I crunched on a mouthful of ice chips. I'd just finished sipping my second tall glass of lemon Coke in an hour. Pepper sat right beside me, pretending to be captivated by the bartender telling a dirty joke. One delicate hand played with her vodka straight up with a lime twist, while the other massaged my inner thigh.

Feeling the sweat prickling on my forehead, I squinted up at the hands on the clock mounted high on the wall between shelves of hard liquor and cold cases of beer. I sneered, disappointed that Sokolov hadn't shown up yet. Time for solving this case was draining faster than sand through an hourglass.

My body convulsed at Pepper's fingers squeezed my crotch in a passionate grip. "Ready to check into a suite?" she said, eager to seduce me again.

"Not yet. I've got to talk with this tattoo artist. He might know why Dee-Dee was killed."

"Alright. Fine." Pepper released my balls and patted my leg. She hopped off her seat. Difficult to tell if she was as bored as I was, or pissed that I wasn't interested in her right now. "I'm going to the ladies room," she told me, then bopped away, her curvy behind igniting a trail of lust that turned heads.

"Another Coke, sir?" the bartender said, removing my glass.

I shuddered with doubt and fatigue. Sir? He had to be kidding. In the crowd of reserved patrons who wore tailored clothes off the rack from Men's Warehouse or Nordstrom, I was wearing bleached, patched-up jeans and a white, coffee-stained T-shirt that read *Stay the Course* in black calligraphy script. "No. The last two glasses tasted kinda funny. Too sweet. Not enough carbonation, maybe? Just black coffee, thanks."

"Coming right up." He scooted down the bar, barely pausing at a hand with an assortment of bling on fingers with manicured, claw-like nails that waved a pair of fifty dollar bills.

Flinging squeezed lemon wedges off the cocktail napkin beside the soaked coaster, I wiped my perspiring face down. When the bartender returned with my java, I intended to tell him to turn the heat down or the air conditioner up.

Pepper was taking too long in the ladies room.

The nerves around my eyes started to twitch. My five-dollar coffee arrived in a dainty, gold-trimmed cup. I took a sip of the steaming brew, feeling the hot liquid trickle down into my stomach. It burned, and a sour taste rushed upward into my throat. I cupped a shaky hand over my mouth and slid off the stool, my feet hitting the tiled floor as if it were quicksand wanting to suck me in over my head. I latched onto the edge of the bar to hold myself upright. Beads of sweat rolling down my cheeks, I swallowed the puke, then staggered out of the lounge.

Blinking at an opaque mist that was creeping into my peripheral vision, I peered around the main lobby, then stumbled against the arboretum, pressing my palms against the glass for balance. As I scanned the lobby slowly in search of a sign indicating the restrooms, a gang of tattooed Goths floated past me like apparitions, ignoring my pleas for help.

I gaped as the ink burst out of their skins in blots and swirls. U of O's green and yellow Fighting Duck on a dude's massive biceps heckled me with quacks. Chinese throwing stars popped from a bed of lotus blossoms decorating another guy's sleeve to twirl at my head. I raised my arms to block, bent my knees to dodge. Cruel laughter flooded my ears, drawing me down a discombobulating whirlpool. A fairy pinup sporting a flailing dragon's tail on a girl's lower back winked, then toasted me with a sip from a martini in its taloned hand. The liquid spewed back out in a singeing flame.

Pepper's face appeared in my hallucinogenic haze, her expression terrified. "What the hell's wrong with you?"

"Drugged, poisoned," I rasped. "Need to get—emergency room . . ."

Her hands braced my shoulders. "Can you walk?"

I nodded sluggishly. Her hand seized mine, and Pepper rushed us toward the main entrance, where the Goths with animated tats milled about. "No, no, no!" I pulled back. "Fire exit."

"This way. There's one around the corner from the restrooms."

My glassy sight swimming through a perpetual blur, I made out the clock behind the registration desk—just a few minutes away from the top of the witching hour. We took a sharp right, moved a few yards down a wide hallway of convention room doors where the view became telescopic. She abruptly yanked me into a passageway that twisted and turned through a maze. "Almost there."

As I began to fall Pepper wrapped an arm around my waist, pulled my arm over her shoulders, and dragged me forward. "Hang on, Matt." With her free hand she pushed a crash bar that opened with a heavy click. The air beyond the door smelled stuffy. The EXIT sign above the double doors twenty yards down the corridor shone brightly.

Just I little farther, I told my rubbery legs.

Halfway there, the double doors at the end flew open.

Two pudgy guys, one in jeans and a turtleneck sweater, the other wearing tan slacks and a Hawaiian-print, short-sleeved button-down shirt, blocked the archway. Turning my head toward the direction we'd come from, I glimpsed two more men in pleated slacks, starched white shirts, and leather jackets sauntering in. I recognized one as the kickboxer from Leslie's gym—the contender who looked forward to a rematch with her. I was certain he'd settle for one round with me. "Ahhh shit," I slurred, "they'll let any asshole in this hotel."

The snickering dude next to the kickboxer pulled a set of shiny brass knuckles out of his suit coat pocket, fitted them over his right hand, then curled up a fist. A clanging sound brought my attention back to the two goons impeding our escape. The guy to the left swung a meat hook on the end of a chain to and fro, while the fella beside him triggered a stun gun, the prongs discharging a flash that raised the short hairs on the back of my neck.

I pushed Pepper aside gently, then closed an eye, pretending to give her a wink. Dropping to one knee, I drew the baby Glock from the ankle holster I'd strapped on back at the gas station, then sighted down the barrel to aim and shoot—only a black hand with talon-like nails clutched my wrist. The demonic paw wrestled my arm downward and shook the gun from my grasp. Straining my muscles to regain control, I looked up into the fearsome, glowing eyes of a growling specter. Its protruding tongue sprouted goosebumps on my skin.

Hearing the whoosh as a blade came slicing at my throat, I blocked the forearm brandishing the scimitar, then seized the thing's wrist before it could attack again. A third appendage on the luscious female body protruded to hold Dee-Dee Magnolia's severed head right up to my face. Shocked by the grotesque trophy, I didn't see the fourth arm swinging until it caught me on the side of my head with a haymaker that sent me sprawling across the cold concrete floor on my stomach.

Flipping over, I wailed through chattering teeth as an electrical charge surged at my abdominal muscles, sending my nerves into spasms. "Come As You Are," the ringtone for Leslie on my mobile, was drowned out by my staccato heartbeat as the four henchmen circled around me. The kickboxer struck my jaw with his heel, just before the others trampled me down into darkness.

TWELVE

Leslie Crow

DARKNESS SHROUDED the fire-gutted church near the junction of Southeast Divers and Porter Roads on Squaw Mountain in Estacada. Nighttime in the country was the ideal place for isolation, privacy, and the blackness of revenge that consumed a piece of my soul with each passing moment that Dee's murder remained unsolved. Fat drops of rain began spattering my windshield as I turned into the modest gravel parking area next to the ruin. The only way I could still tell it had been a place of worship was the iron cross mounted at the top of the steeple still rising from the center.

Right away, a casual observation told me something was off.

My Saturn wasn't the only vehicle in the lot. A black limousine took up five spaces, while a silver Lincoln had double-parked beside it to make getting out difficult. Rocks crunching under radials, I pulled the Saturn around and parked near the lot entrance. Heavy winds ruffled the thick anchorage of pine and fir trees in the field across the road.

Digging my iPhone out of the inside pocket of my duster coat, I read the time on the screensaver: just past 12:45 a.m. There was no voicemail or text from Matt, asking me to check in or updating me on how his meeting with Dan went. Back at the morgue, seeing a fresh body being wheeled in hadn't helped to suppress my mounting concerns.

Especially when the ME unzipped the bag and I identified Derek Sharp.

A thin cut had sawed through his throat where he'd been garroted, probably with a length of piano wire. Round ligature marks pressed into the flesh around the wound couldn't be identified precisely by the ME, but Goldman presumed that maybe the strangling instrument was concealed in a strand of jewelry, like a pearl necklace.

Leaving Green Beans to gather clues from the dead, I'd made a pit stop at Femme Ink to check there myself, since Matt hadn't uncovered any leads at the crime scene. Running short on time, I focused my search on Dee's station. Her sketchbook filled with artwork she'd already tattooed, works in progress, or designs she intended to ink someday was gone.

I received a new e-mail, but it wasn't from Matt, as I'd hoped. It was an e-card from Dee. Mind reeling, I tapped the message open. The postcard graphic of the Yaquina Head Lighthouse prodded my memory of our visit there.

A burst of thunder, following a lightning flash that cast a strobe of light over the terrain, interrupted my unraveling thoughts. The loud clap didn't drown out the gunshot that cracked inside the church.

Pushing the compartment between the seats open, I snagged my black leather gloves and put them on. I got out of the car and bolted for the church entrance. Hopping and skipping over charred debris from the fire, I reached the bottom of the steps, the Glock raised one-handed to cover my twelve o'clock. The flames that'd eaten away at the wood and concrete had been so intense and ravenous, they'd singed the branches and trunks of an elm tree in the front yard that reached up to the bell tower. Lightning pulsed again to throw light and shadows from the torched elm's gnarled limbs against the double doors of the church, now looking like a yawning mouth bordered by jagged teeth after firefighters had chopped their way in with axes.

I saw the shiny loafers of a body lying just beyond the splintered arch.

I slowly climbed the five wide steps to reach the corpse. Mother Nature's light show paused long enough for my sight to adjust to the darkness as I squatted over the well-dressed man, and I saw the fresh bloody holes stitched in his chest and stomach. His eastern European features and expensive threads matched those of the men Matt and I had spotted outside Femme Ink the night Dee was murdered.

Not bothering to check for a pulse, I moved forward, staying low. The stench of gunpowder grew thicker and combined with the sour stench of soot to make my gut retch. Black bean hummus didn't taste good trying to come back up. I stepped through the foyer, my shoes crunching on blackened iron hangers strewn about that must've been stored in a coat closet on my right, where the charcoaled door hung by a hinge.

I entered the church proper and gasped at the hollowed-out remains. What cinders of pews remained had been tossed aside. Rainwater dripped from leaks in the joints and timbers of the structure. Goldman had informed me that forensic evidence told him the three teenage girls found in the building were alive while the flames consumed the church.

A noise toward the back, behind the altar and pulpit, tripped my reflexes to aim the Glock in that general direction. I shuffled around more debris and climbed up onto the pulpit dais. A man's robust body was curled into a fetal position before me. He was clutching his pot belly tightly with both hands, as blood seeped through his fingers. The knuckles of his right hand were scraped and swollen from striking someone recently.

Among other things he'd confessed to me, Goldman told me that at around 11:00 p.m., representatives of the Russian Government had paid him a visit. They were there to take possession of one of the dead girls. When Goldman balked at their request, wanting to preserve evidence in a high-profile investigation, one of them punched him in the eye.

I didn't feel sorry for the pathetic son of a bitch. When I'd signed in for my visitor's pass to see him, I'd noticed Dee's signature scrawled in several lines above mine. The date and time indicated she'd been to the morgue last Friday morning. I asked Goldman about it. After humming and hawing, the prick admitted calling her in to identify one of the girls from the fire because of a tat he'd found on the body. The ink had tried to conceal a strawberry-shaped birthmark on the shoulder. Dee had been furious when she recognized the tattoo as originating from her scrapbook.

Sudden clarity widened my eyes. I knew where Dee had stashed her artwork for safekeeping. At the lighthouse's museum and visitor center she'd chuckled at a recreation of the keeper's sleeping quarters from the turn of the century—namely, the books by John Grisham and Stephen King on the shelves to help them pass the time on their watches. She would've inserted her book there, in plain sight.

Hearing a whoosh of water behind me that sounded nothing like the pouring rain outside or inside, I shot a look over my shoulder. The outline of a nun's habit appeared in the baptism chamber window behind the pulpit. A muzzle where her hand could've been rose, flashed. The bullet chipped the weathered pulpit, exploding splinters into my hair.

I swayed backward, dodged a snap shot that would've perforated a lung. Sprinting forward, I extended the Glock sideways to pump five rounds into the baptism chamber. A groan sounded, followed by a splash, then a thump on wood. I advanced on the target zone, the gun raised in a two-handed grip for a sure kill if the bitch in the box popped back up again.

The only sounds I heard were my heart hammering inside my chest and *drip ... drip ... drip.*

Yelling like a banshee, the enraged figure cloaked in the drenched habit sprang up and leapt through the shattered window, hands extended. Her claws gripped my shoulders, her weight spun me around, and we took a dive into the air off the dais.

Hitting the ground on my hip, I heard my gun skitter across the floor. I gave the sister a head butt that released her handhold on me, then rolled away to push up sideways, looking around for my piece. The click of a switchblade directed my focus to the assassin's fist as lightning glinted on the blade preceding another thunderclap.

As the assassin twirled the blade around, I watched the madness in her eyes and recalled the ME's findings from the autopsy report on Dee that he'd allowed me to glance through: *The victim was strangled pre-mortem. The bruises on her neck bear this out. However, the lack of hemorrhaging in the eyes tells me she died from the dozen stab wounds inflicted to her torso.*

"Is that what you used on Dee-Dee?" I asked, leaping back to evade a thrust.

"Not me. I prefer slitting my prey's throat to bleeding them like a stuck pig. That's how the slut—"

The assassin found it hard to finish after I wove around the knife, locked her elbow in an arm bar to incapacitate the blade, then rammed my knee up into her stomach. The crucifix dangling from a string of prayer beads around her neck got my attention. Grabbing the strand, I spun around to get behind her and dragged her arm still grasping the knife up between her shoulder blades.

I separated a gap between the beads under her larynx with a thumb and forefinger, felt the taut wire, then twisted the strand of beads again and again to tighten the crude noose.

The assassin gagged and struggled. I jammed a knee into her lower back to hold her steady while I notched up the pressure.

"Your disguise really *pisses* me off," I growled into her ear. "Nuns would beat my mother up the side of the head for speaking in her native tongue. Speaking of tongue, what color is yours right now?"

I heard a gurgle and released the assassin to shove her forward. Her body struck the floor like a slab of cordwood, a pool of blood oozing from the wound in her throat I'd sliced open with the piano wire. I found my weapon and picked it up.

I didn't expect to find anything useful, but I gave her a pat-down anyway. A cell phone I found inside the robe provided a hit. A text informed me that the second half of the assassin's payment was waiting in a mailbox at an address outside the Carver Curves.

Dee's homestead.

●

LIGHTS OFF (which included pulling the fuse for the running lights), I shifted the Saturn into neutral and coasted down the driveway. I leaned forward, seatbelt unfastened, eyes darting side-to-side, on the lookout for sentries and ready to leap out when one caught me entering. An ominous feeling told me this route for sneaking in was suicide and I'd get my head blown off for sure.

I pulled in next to the barn and got out. Inhaling deeply to muster my strength, I pushed and steered the Saturn about twenty feet into the high grass. Then, head down, I jogged for the fence line in back. Matt's screams from within made me flinch and tense up for a second. I moved faster and hurdled over the fence.

I stopped dead, glaring at the back of a guard slouched against the left side of the large entrance to the stables. Holding my breath, I tiptoed up to him, drew the Glock from the shoulder sling underneath my duster coat, and stabbed the barrel against the back of his skull. "How many of you are there?" I whispered.

His head tipped sideways as if weighing his options.

"Talk," I said, pushing the muzzle harder.

The sentry fell over onto his back. I crouched down to probe for injuries. Rubbing fingers over the vertebrae behind his neck, I felt the shattered bones beneath the skin. His neck had been broken with skill and severe torque.

Under cover of more screams, I ran into the stables. Hammer was kicking at his stall, so I holstered my gun, but something or someone else was spooking the hell out of him. Climbing the slats on the stall next to his, I hugged the square post and scrambled up the coarse surface. I stepped onto the loft and peeked out over the main floor.

The savages had Matt suspended naked two feet off the ground, his wrists clasped in handcuffs, which in turn dangled from a meat hook fastened to a chain run through the pulley. A tall man with milk chocolate skin and long fingers snickered, holding a cattle prod to Matt's balls. A whiz of urine spurted to soak up and down the body of a kickboxer I knew from my gym.

"Ah, shit!" the henchman complained. "May I be excused so I can clean up?"

"Yes, but come right back." The albino bombshell flicked a lighter, then blew a dainty stream of richly scented tobacco smoke at Matt.

"There are infinite ways I can make you suffer," she promised. "I can cut you a thousand times, but the last thing I want is to mutilate the artwork on your body. Maybe I'll rip the piercings out of your face and nipples. You have until I finish this smoke to furnish the names, then I'm going to plug the juice in until your eyeballs *pop*."

I took the time to shift around and observe the kickboxer walking between the stables. This would be it. He'd spot the dead sentry for sure, raise the alarm, and while they'd scour the ranch for me, I could pull Matt up. I grabbed a length of dusty rope and began tying it off through the chain connection.

Pepper stepped into view, cocking a thumb over her shoulder. My hands shook with fright, watching Pepper leap onto the kickboxer to wrap her legs around his chest, box his ears, then ride him down hard into the concrete floor. Holding him securely with her bulging thighs, Pepper wrapped both arms around his head to pull it sternly into her boobs with a vicious twist.

Crunch!

Holy shit, I mouthed.

Drawing my weapon, I watched Pepper doing the same as she walked out across the main floor. Pointing the baby Glock

I'd given to Matt years ago, she put a slug in the eye of the African American brandishing the prod. His blood spurted across Matt's ribs. Aim level and smooth, she pointed the compact at the albino babe, who didn't so much as blink.

Like an heiress that'd been spoiled all her life, she merely shrugged. "What, Pepper?"

"You should have stuck to the plan. Dee would've taken the money."

"She met with the medical examiner to identify one of the bodies of our returned merchandise. The setup failed." The albino swiveled her head to blow more smoke.

"Look at me, Misha. I'll never ask you a more important question again in your life. Did you piece together that Dee's mentor was instrumental in putting your father away?"

A cold silence stretched between Pepper and the older woman, a dead silence similar to what I'd felt in my loft the night of Dee's murder.

"Yes!" the albino shouted gleefully. "I killed that stoner bitch. If not for her teacher, my father wouldn't have rotted in prison, and maybe the ATF wouldn't have seized my inheritance."

Pepper pulled the trigger until the magazine emptied, dyeing the albino's hair with a red, misty mop of her own gore.

It awakened Matt from the state they'd sedated him into. "Jesus H. Christ, Pepper!" he shouted. "What the fuck happened to you?"

Dangling the smoking gun at her side for a moment before she released it, she turned around to face Matt. "It's a long story," she said. "Let's just say I fell in league with the wrong people, became a slave, worked my way back up out of the pit I landed in, became an enforcer, and now . . . I'm more or less a plant to draw out the monsters who buy flesh."

"By supplying the demand."

"If you're fishing for sharks," Pepper said in a hushed tone, put off by his naïveté, "you can't use sardines for bait."

"You're part of the problem, not the solution," Matt yelled. "Can't you see that?"

"Fuck you, Matt. Fuck you! I survived as one of those sex slaves for two years, so don't guilt me into any 'poor me' trips. You have no fucking idea what's worse here—the criminals selling skin for cash, or the animals that rape you. I lost a child, you asshole. One way or another, everyone's going to pay."

I squeezed off a fine shot that grazed Pepper's biceps. Yelping, she cupped a hand over the flesh wound.

"Step away from him," I said, "or the next one's going right through your mouth."

"Hey, Leslie. Still a bad-ass, I see," Pepper called out.

"Shut the hell up and move back."

She did, alright, while managing to keep Matt's hanging body in the line of fire so I couldn't get a clean shot.

"You wanna know something?" she said, throwing her voice from the huge doors. "My new mission in life has taught me so many vital life skills." Reaching into a box on top of a work bench, she withdrew a flare and struck the tip. "For instance . . ." She paused, tilting her head to admire the burning light as if it were a falling star, "sanitizing a crime scene." Pepper hurled the flare up into the loft before she ran out.

The stick of dribbling phosphorous landed on top of the wall of bales I was using for cover. The straw burst into flame. I took a few steps back, then ran across the loft, flames trailing after the soles of my boots. Leaping out into space, I clutched the chain Matt dangled from and climbed down hand-under-hand. Hanging right behind him, I held onto the chain with one hand, while fishing my handcuffs skeleton key out of my duster coat.

The heat of the fire made him sweat buckets; his wrists kept sliding around inside the bracelets. "Hold still," I said, baring my teeth in frustration.

The chain was warming like an extra-hot cup of coffee without a sleeve. A small explosion rained burning straw.

I dropped the damn key.

Pulling a bobby pin I kept in my jeans pocket for emergencies, I went to work on the lock. "Come on, you mother . . ."

Hearing the soft click, I yanked the bracelets apart for Matt to drop. He hit the ground on his knees in a sticky mess of blood, sweat, and urine. The heels of my boots touched down close by, and I helped him up, then reeled around, looking for an escape. The fire crackled and licked along the side walls and the rafters.

"Come on!" I yanked him along. "Move!"

At Hammer's stall, I stopped to lean Matt up against a post, then pulled the latch to Hammer's gate open and jumped back. Whinnying in a frenzy of preservation, Hammer jammed out, his hooves clacking across the asphalt. Matt and I followed suit, not nearly as quick, hacking up lungfuls of carbon dioxide.

A few steps outside the entrance, Matt sniffed the air. "What's that stink?"

"You," I said, giving him a wry grin.

"No." He took another whiff. "Oh God, it's you. You're on fire!"

I pulled the smoldering wool coat off and tossed it back into the barn as the loft came crashing down.

Unfastening the gate, I swung it out, then watched Hammer gallop away to safety. Shivering in the wind, rain showering his nude, beaten body, Matt stared at the blaze, haunted by the truth he wanted going up in smoke. With a sullen look of disbelief myself, I dug my iPhone out of my pocket.

Once I'd finished the 911 call, I sauntered over to Matt and said, "Come on, partner, let's wait in the car where it's dry, before you catch a pneumonia."

EPILOGUE

Leslie Crow

LISTENING TO GPS directions through my Bluetooth, I steered my sleek blue and silver Honda X11 Streetfighter through the teeming streets of the Castro District. Vistas of thick gray clouds that'd delivered a solid rainfall earlier scudded before variable winds that made for a slick, exhilarating ride. The late-morning sunlight burning through the thick fog cover from the bay made everything sparkle. I throttled up a steep hill and relished the surge of the engine accelerating between my legs.

I felt as free-spirited as the seagulls I spotted hovering around Coit Tower.

The husky voice of a flirtatious girl I'd selected to be my GPS narrator said, "You've arrived at your destination, gorgeous."

I caught the blink of taillights and a puff of exhaust from the tailpipe ahead of me and waited, then swerved into a parking spot vacated by a maroon Prius three storefronts up from the Boogie Clay Crafts and Gifts head shop. Switching the engine off, I set the kick stand and dismounted to pull off the full-face helmet and set it down on the front of the bike. Unzipping my leather jacket to allow my skin to breathe, I shifted the messenger bag slung from my shoulder from my lower back down to my hip. Stepping over the stew of leaves in the gutter and onto the cracked sidewalk, I moseyed past the storefront window, studying the colorful display of handmade pottery that ranged from change dishes and mushroom incense burners to coffee mugs and vases. The top shelf featured round candy bowls modeled to look like carved pumpkins. A flyer in the lower corner of the window near the entrance announced the Castro Street Fair that always takes place on the first Sunday of October.

I opened the glass door and stepped inside. Nicotine smoke and fragrant incense wafted around the sales floor. The Stones played from a CD changer in the left corner behind the counter. I looked to my right and saw a man carefully cleaning a wooden shelf lined with champagne flutes and wine goblets with a feather duster. He stood in profile to me.

He took a puff from an American Spirit cigarette and blew out a thick smoke ring. His light brown goatee and mustache couldn't hide a devilish grin of contentment. He placed the cigarette in an ashtray on a nearby table, his silver ponytail swinging gracefully between his shoulder blades. He wore baggy denim jeans and a beige corduroy button-down shirt with the sleeves rolled up to show off muscular forearms that hadn't lost any tone from surfing.

I bolted the door, pulled its shade down, and also closed the storefront window blinds. Muscles tensing at the room's dimming, he whipped around to face me.

"Hello, Dah-nee-l."

Tucking the duster in his back pocket, he took a pack of smokes out of his shirt pocket, and even though the other one still smoldered, he stuck a fresh one between his lips. He struck the head of a wooden match with a thumbnail, lit the cig, and took a deep drag. "I remember you," Dee's mentor said. "The last time I saw you, though, you had braces and wore feathers in your pigtails."

I couldn't help but grin at that faded memory from my youth. I didn't smile often these days.

His expression shifted from "glad to see you" to paranoid in a heartbeat. "What are you doing here, Leslie?"

I unclasped the flap of my shoulder bag and opened it. Removing a heart-shaped box, I flipped the magnetized lid open and revealed the powdery contents sealed in a plastic Baggie. "Dee's ashes. She stipulated in her will that she wanted me to deliver them to you personally."

"Thank you," Dan said, sticking the cigarette in a corner of his mouth before accepting the remains. "Did you get them?"

"All but one. Her protégé got away."

"What did Pepper do?"

"Human traffickers she worked with stole one of Dee's designs and used it to conceal a birthmark on a girl they sold."

A teardrop trailed down the crags of his face as he pinched his tear ducts. "I'd warned her being a Samaritan could lead to being used. There's no one easier to abuse than a person who wears her heart on her sleeve." He gently set the box down next to the ashtray.

"There's something else I need your help with," I said, pulling the messenger bag strap over my head and my jacket off to let them drop to the floor. I untucked my Jefferson Airplane T-shirt to peel it off and tossed it on the pile. Turning my back toward Dan, I unhooked my bra.

He uttered a foreign word in his deep baritone that made me week in the knees.

"What did you say?"

"'Beautiful' in Ukrainian. Is it okay if I touch?"

"Yes," I said, then felt his rough fingertips tenderly caress my skin and the back piece tattoo Dee had inked the weekend we spent in Newport. Surrounded by a dreamcatcher, the outline showed my mother as a teenager, a soothing hand on her massive belly pregnant with me, another shielding her eyes from a blazing sky to gaze out across the plains. "It needs coloring."

"I wouldn't think of doing that," he said, "unless you have Dee-Dee's original sketch."

"In the satchel," I told him, nodding down at the bag. "Name any price you want."

He placed a consoling hand on my shoulder. "For you I will, but not for money. This way." He walked me through a curtain of beads into a compact parlor in the back.

Dan put on a pair of bifocals and waved downward at a tattoo chair. Wiggling my breasts against the cushion to get comfortable, I got a whiff of the pungent sanitizer Dan washed his hands with. He squirted tepid water on my back and gently scrubbed all over from the tip of my spine down to my tailbone, then dried me off with a soft terrycloth towel. Rubber gloves stretched and snapped.

The tattoo machine hummed, the steady sting of the needles piercing my nerve fibers with a sharp pain more hurtful than the tears I finally shed. But it felt good just the same, relinquishing the grip on my sorrow.

Acknowledgments

With special thanks to:

Jordan Dane and the other authors and participants at The Kill Zone blog for their critique and guidance in polishing the prologue.

Nick Slosser for his encouragement and criticism keeping me honest.

Marg Gilks for infusing the words with a resonant beat.

Bobbi Steele for her generous counsel and wisdom.

Allison McDonough for sharing stories about her tattoos and maintaining the finest, independent coffee shop in Portland. Your ink makes this story more authentic, while the atmosphere and courteous baristas in the Green Beans Coffee and Tea shop furnish a second home for my imagination to thrive in.

My wife, Kim, for paying the biggest compliment to Matt and Leslie. One night we're driving home from dinner and I'm telling her about a breakthrough in character development or the plot, and after she agrees with me, or cautions me not to over think it, she says, 'Isn't it *weird* how we talk about these characters sometimes like they're real people?'

I'm thankful to have a beloved wife who understands me and this storytelling craft I'm addicted to.

About the Author

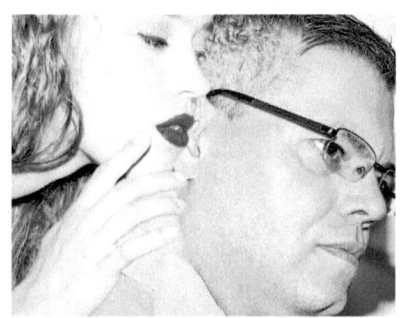

A Portland native, Aaron Hilton has worked at a video store, in a mail room, accounts payable, security, and for fifteen years, as an alarm control operator for Fred Meyer and Kroger. He enjoys digital photography, film noir, pin-ups, scary movies, sequential art, and strong coffee.

He is currently writing the next book in the Alternative Investigations series.

Photographer Credit: Angelique Herrington

www.ingramcontent.com/pod-product-compliance
Lightning Source LLC
Chambersburg PA
CBHW050942120626
46552CB00001B/340